"THIS NONSENSE ABOUT THE FEUD HAS GONE ON FAR TOO LONG.

"Our families are just going to have to accept the way we feel about each other," Lucas said firmly. "Pa took the news very well."

Coldly, she demanded, "But why shouldn't he? He probably figures you're just getting me out of your system."

"What is that supposed to mean?"

"Just what it sounds like. For all your father knows, you're just sowing a few wild oats. Of course he approves. In fact, I'll bet he thinks it's great that you're doing it with a Hanlon."

Lucas's hard hands tightened on her. He loomed over her, big and angry and unrestrainedly masculine. "So you think I'm just using you, is that it?" he asked. "Let me tell you something, lady. I sowed all the wild oats I needed to a long time ago. You should be grateful I didn't do it with you."

A CANDLELIGHT ECSTASY ROMANCE®

250 SUMMER WINE, *Alexis Hill Jordan*
251 NO LOVE LOST, *Eleanor Woods*
252 A MATTER OF JUDGMENT, *Emily Elliott*
253 GOLDEN VOWS, *Karen Whittenburg*
254 AN EXPERT'S ADVICE, *Joanne Bremer*
255 A RISK WORTH TAKING, *Jan Stuart*
256 GAME PLAN, *Sara Jennings*
257 WITH EACH PASSING HOUR, *Emma Bennett*
258 PROMISE OF SPRING, *Jean Hager*
259 TENDER AWAKENING, *Alison Tyler*
260 DESPERATE YEARNING, *Dallas Hamlin*
261 GIVE AND TAKE, *Sheila Paulos*
262 AN UNFORGETTABLE CARESS, *Donna Kimel Vitek*
263 TOMORROW WILL COME, *Megan Lane*
264 RUN TO RAPTURE, *Margot Prince*
265 LOVE'S SECRET GARDEN, *Nona Gamel*
266 WINNER TAKES ALL, *Cathie Linz*
267 A WINNING COMBINATION, *Lori Copeland*
268 A COMPROMISING PASSION, *Nell Kincaid*
269 TAKE MY HAND, *Anna Hudson*
270 HIGH STAKES, *Eleanor Woods*
271 SERENA'S MAGIC, *Heather Graham*
272 A DARING ALLIANCE, *Alison Tyler*
273 SCATTERED ROSES, *Jo Calloway*
274 WITH ALL MY HEART, *Emma Bennett*
275 JUST CALL MY NAME, *Dorothy Ann Bernard*
276 THE PERFECT AFFAIR, *Lynn Patrick*
277 ONE IN A MILLION, *Joan Grove*
278 HAPPILY EVER AFTER, *Barbara Andrews*
279 SINNER AND SAINT, *Prudence Martin*
280 RIVER RAPTURE, *Patricia Markham*
281 MATCH MADE IN HEAVEN, *Malissa Carroll*

LOVE NOT THE ENEMY

Sara Jennings

A CANDLELIGHT ECSTASY ROMANCE®

Published by
Dell Publishing Co., Inc.
1 Dag Hammarskjold Plaza
New York, New York 10017

ISBN: 0-440-15070-1

Printed in the United States of America
First printing—November 1984

To Our Readers:

We have been delighted with your enthusiastic response to Candlelight Ecstasy Romances®, and we thank you for the interest you have shown in this exciting series.

In the upcoming months we will continue to present the distinctive, sensuous love stories you have come to expect only from Ecstasy. We look forward to bringing you many more books from your favorite authors and also the very finest work from new authors of contemporary romantic fiction.

As always, we are striving to present the unique, absorbing love stories that you enjoy most—books that are more than ordinary romance.

Your suggestions and comments are always welcome. Please write to us at the address below.

Sincerely,

The Editors
Candlelight Romances
1 Dag Hammarskjold Plaza
New York, New York 10017

CHAPTER ONE

South of Parkersburg, near where the Kanawha crosses the state line and becomes West Virginia's New River, Carly Hanlon turned toward home.

Off Route 77, away from the long, rumbling trucks and darting cars, the bright neon lights of roadside cafes and the tumbledown buildings of better times no one could really remember, she headed southeast into the night and the mountains, seeking the way home.

There were easier ways to get there, but they didn't appeal to her. Going home shouldn't be easy. Not after ten years away and a lifetime of new experiences to separate her from all she had once known and been.

Home. The word had a hollow ring, promising much but guaranteeing nothing.

"When you comin' home, Carly?" Ma had asked.

"Soon. I promise. Maybe Christmas."

How many visits half intended, pushed aside in the whirl of the new world she wanted so desperately to make her own?

"When you comin' home, Carly?" Pa had written. "We miss you."

I know. I ache inside too. Just because I don't come back doesn't mean I don't care. Can't you tell I'm scared?

But they could tell, the mountain people, who lived with fear as a birthright. They knew the contours of it, the ebb and flow, and all the tricks of coexisting with the big, endless question of, "Oh, Lord, what next?"

"You won't be comin' home, Carly," Lucas Murdock had said that last night ten years ago when they happened across each other on the far side of the lake. She had been on Murdock land, where she had no call to be but had gone in a final gesture of defiance against everything that was sending her away.

"Don't you tell me what I'll be doin'. I'd as soon listen to the wind as a Murdock."

He'd laughed at that, the rich, knowing laugh she hated. Easy for him to laugh. Rich by valley standards, handsome as the devil, college educated. Wild, they called him, and maybe they were right.

Standing there in the moonlight pouring off Whisper Mountain with the lake water lapping at their feet and the hoot owls calling, he'd looked at her in a way that made her yearn for the wildness, if only for a moment.

"Easy for you to talk," she'd protested, knowing there was more to object to than just his arrogance. Temptation, get thee behind me.

Bound for the great world beyond, for knowledge and position, no mere man was going to make her step from the chosen path. "I hear you aren't stickin' around. Off to some fancy law school over east, aren't you?"

"Now how did you know that, Carly Hanlon? 'Less you make it your business to ask about me?"

She'd flushed at that even though it wasn't true. She

was very careful never to mention his name, even turning away when it came up round the counter of Mr. Pearson's General Store or Maybelle Lane's Beauty Parlor.

He was trouble. She'd known that as long as she'd known anything. "Stay clear of the Murdocks," Ma had said. "They've bad blood."

As a child she'd tried to picture that, imagining the red flow of life contaminated in some awful way. Such a surprise that day at the mine when Lucas had gone to help men trapped below from a cavein and had come up with part of his right arm crushed. His blood was as red as any other man's and every bit as hot and sticky on her novice hands as she'd prayed to remember everything she'd learned in that first-aid course given over at the church.

"You've got no call helpin' a Murdock," Pa had said later when he heard of it.

"I had to, he was hurt bad."

"You're always reachin' out to the sick and injured, Carly. That's a fine tendency in a woman, bodes well for her family to come. But you've got to restrain it sometimes. Murdocks are trouble."

Why, Pa?

She'd never asked the question. It would have been like questioning the color of the sky or the passage of migrating birds or the endless round of seasons.

Murdocks were, had always been, and would always be bad. There was nothing else to it.

Rain was slapping against the windshield of the jeep. She turned the wipers to a faster speed and peered out at the darkness. There had been a time when she could see well by the dimmest starlight, finding her way through wood and glen like the night creatures she loved to watch.

She'd lost that skill in the big city, along with a few

other things. But she was bringing back with her a vast world of knowledge, even of so wondrous a miracle as how her green eyes shot through with rays of gold had once been able to penetrate the thickest darkness.

She understood the physiology of it now, the secret inner life of cell and synapse. Was that true compensation for no longer having the night vision itself?

Maybe she could get it back. The thought pleased her and she smiled, brushing away a strand of the chestnut hair that had fallen across her cheek. The piles of luggage in the backseat partially obscured the rearview mirror.

She was tempted to pull over and rearrange them. But at night on a narrow, rain-slicked road that could be daring fate. Better to keep on and hope for the best.

Pa had laughed when she warned him how much stuff she was bringing back, not just clothes and books, but equipment and supplies for the practice she was going to start. "We'll make room, honey. Just you bring yourself too. Hear?"

Yes, Pa, I hear. The sound of understanding and forgiveness is sweet on my soul.

Ten years away, almost a stranger. Yet still family, still the daughter to be welcomed back. Coming home at last, bringing the great dream with her, an offering of love.

It wasn't going to be easy; she didn't kid herself about that. Plenty of people would look sharply at what she had done, and at what she now was.

Refrain from judgment, she pleaded silently as she slowed down to take a particularly tight curve. Just give me a chance, that's all I ask. A chance for all of us.

The road was climbing upward. A box rattled in the back; syringes, it sounded like. She hoped nothing was getting broken. There hadn't been much money to spend.

She'd parceled it out in little bits, wanting the most for every penny.

"Are you really sure this is what you want to do?" Frank had asked at the party they'd all gone to in celebration of the end of residency.

She'd looked at him in surprise. How could she answer a question that erroneously presumed she had a choice in the matter?

"Middle-class America can get along without me," she'd said at last, gently so as not to hurt him. Frank was headed for a practice that would make him a wealthy man. He wanted that almost as much as he wanted to be a doctor. But she didn't.

"Then go to work in one of the ghettos," he'd suggested. "Bed-Stuy, Watts, people there are desperate for help."

"So are people in Spruce Hollow."

He'd frowned, not truly believing. To him, poor people were black or brown and lived in slums. She knew better.

True, grinding poverty, the kind that saps all hope and kills young, knew no color and often dwelt in the loveliest places on God's green earth, amid rolling hills and verdant forests, down lonely back roads where those who didn't want to know didn't have to go.

Places like Spruce Hollow. Home, haven, prison. She was an escapee returning with the key held tight in her hand. That little bit of the world, which had once been all the world, inspired her love and hatred in equal measure.

Funny how Lucas Murdock had seemed to understand. They seemed so different on the surface. He big and strong, with hair the color of spilled ink and eyes like blue crystal chips; muscled in the way of a man who does hard, physical work, even if only by choice, lithe with the grace of confidence, virile to a degree that set her heart to thumping and turned her into a fearful doe confronted by a stag.

Next to him, she felt small, which annoyed her since she was anything but. Tall for a woman and strong in her own way, she had a slenderness without fragility.

There were only four years between them, yet he'd known the world far from Spruce Hollow at a time when she could only yearn to reach out to it. Known more too, if she was any judge. More than most men ever guessed or had a right to know.

She'd seen that in his eyes; the hunger and the tenderness and the never-stated but always present invitation to let him show her pleasure's path.

That night by the lake she'd come close to going to him. Only one thing had stopped her: the bus ticket under her pillow back home in the room under the eaves where she'd slept since Timmy came along seventeen years before to push her from the cradle.

Something to dream on, Pa had said when he handed it to her. And how right he was. She was going to the dream whole and intact within herself. Leaving nothing for Lucas Murdock to take lightly and then forget.

They were adversaries, not only by virtue of the bad feeling between their families, but in the ancient way of male and female, needing each other and wary of how much the hot blood could burn on a warm night, or a cold one, or any kind in between.

Yet in the end they'd done the same thing: gone away from the hollow and the glen, left the mountains for the far world beyond. Now she was coming back and Lucas . . . ?

She supposed he was a lawyer somewhere, successful no doubt, since he'd had that look of success stamped on him from the beginning. Did he ever think about the place where he'd grown up? Did it haunt him as it did her?

She shook her head, half in rejection of that possibility and half in annoyance at herself. This was not the time to be thinking of Lucas, or of anything except the necessity of keeping her car on the road when all the elements seemed to be conspiring to get her off.

The wind had picked up, lashing heavy rain the wipers could not remove fast enough. She wasn't absolutely sure where she was. The roads she once could have followed blindfolded were now a jumble of almost memories not to be trusted.

Was that the turn up ahead or was she being fooled by the approaching headlights shining through the multitude of raindrops clinging to the windshield? Slowing the car to little more than a crawl, she perilously inched ahead. Even with her high beams on, she was almost blind.

Inwardly she blamed herself for not considering that the storm might worsen. There were worse fates than spending the night in Parkersburg. She could have stayed over until morning and finished the trip in safety instead of being stuck on a mountain road not knowing what to do next.

Staying where she was wouldn't help. On the winding road there was no telling when a car might happen along from the opposite direction. That could be disastrous for them both. Yet to go on under such circumstances . . .

Reaching a decision, she pulled over to the side and put her emergency flashers on, then rooted around in the glove compartment until she found the flashlight.

To open the door on her side, she had to push hard against the wind. Even after ten years she remembered what such storms could be like. Whipping out of the north in late autumn, they tore the last of the leaves from the trees and put winter on everyone's mind with a vengeance.

Despite her warm wool slacks, boots, sweater, and fleecy jacket, Carly still began shivering the moment she stepped from the protection of the jeep. Gripping the flashlight in gloved hands, she started up the road, determined to learn as much of it as she could hold in her mind before trying to drive it.

The turn she had thought was just ahead turned out to be nothing but shadows curving between two old trees. Up a little the roadside fell away into a deep ravine that struck a distant chord of familiarity. She was farther from the Hollow than she'd thought.

Miles to go before I sleep. The Robert Frost poem was whispered in her mind. She was surprised she remembered it, but then memory was a selective thing, as she was discovering.

Back five miles or so she'd taken a turn without a thought, certain she knew where she was going. Perhaps she had, but it wasn't where she'd intended.

Below in the ravine, darkly invisible and revealed only by the wind-tossed slosh of water, was the lake. A wry smile curved her mouth as she paused to wipe away the rain drops chilling her face. She'd done it again. Not even officially home yet and already on Murdock land.

Not that it mattered, she told herself firmly. Old taboos might die hard, but she knew her rights. The road twisting by the lake was public access. Never mind that she was the only Hanlon ever daft enough to use it.

Dimly she wondered what Lucas's father and three brothers were up to. Presumably snug and dry in the big house on the other side of the water whose lights she could faintly see winking at her. Only a fool would be out on such a night.

Laughing sourly at her own inadvertent joke, she trudged on, covering a few more yards before deciding she'd seen all she could safely hope to remember. When she returned to the car, she rolled the window on her side all the way down and stuck her head out to improve her visibility.

Even so, it was tough going. Her shoulder-length hair quickly became a sodden mass pasted to her head and her skin paled from the cold. Taking off her gloves to give herself a better grip on the steering wheel, she soon discovered how hard it was to drive with numb fingers.

Exasperated, she nonetheless persevered until she had covered all the road she had walked over. Pulling over to the side once again, she got out, determined to continue the process that seemed the only safe way to reach the Hollow that night.

But what had worked fine once did not do so again. Barely had she covered a few yards on foot than the sound of another vehicle coming toward her alerted her to danger. Stepping swiftly onto the side of the road, she waved the flashlight back and forth in warning.

The vehicle slowed, but not enough. Whoever was driving misjudged the distance and came closer than he'd intended. Carly had a moment to realize what was about to happen before a large pickup truck came into view, trundling into a large puddle next to her, and sending a sheet of muddy water over her outraged form.

Of all the . . . ! For one of the rare times in her life, she regretted her lack of fluency in profane language. No word she could utter, even silently, adequately described the sheer, unmitigated fury she was feeling.

Coming on top of a long, tension-filled journey of uneasy memories and worries about the future, it was just too much. Staring down at her filthy, sodden clothes, she ached to tear apart limb by limb the insufferable idiot who had done this to her.

And why not? He was coming right at her, having pulled over near the jeep and doubled back on foot to survey what he had done. The darkness and whipping rain obscured him from her sight. Angry, uncaring, determined to get a look at the lout, she turned the flashlight on him.

He stopped and raised an arm, blinking in the sudden glare. A low growl reached her. "Put that damn thing down!"

Carly's arm dropped. She closed her eyes for an instant, praying she was wrong. When she opened them again, it was to discover that of all the mistakes she had made that evening, this was not one of them.

The voice, the walk, the very shape of his body were all achingly familiar, engraved on her mind by some force she did not want to acknowledge.

Lucas Murdock closed the distance between them, his tall, lean body dressed in jeans and a rain slicker that did nothing to disguise the sheer male beauty of his form.

His eyes were sharp as he surveyed her bedraggled state and his smile mocking as he bowed insolently. "The prodigal returns. Welcome home, Dr. Hanlon."

CHAPTER TWO

"If you're the reception committee," Carly muttered, "I'd just as soon pass."

Lucas quirked an eyebrow at her. "What did you expect, a gala celebration? You've been gone a long time."

"Ten years." It was a reminder to herself of everything that had happened since the last time she had seen him. She was no longer a naive young girl with a head stuffed full of dreams. A woman faced him now, sure of herself and her place.

"And two months," he said quietly.

The simple words cut a swath through her hard-won composure. She stared at him in surprise, not wanting to read anything into his unexpected recall. Cautiously, she said, "I could half believe you've been keeping track."

"Only half?"

Grimly, Carly smiled. "I'd forgotten how you like to bandy words, Lucas. But could we pick a drier place for it?"

He laughed with unexpected gentleness. "You do have a point. Where's your car?"

"Down the road a bit. I couldn't see where I was going."

"No kidding?" Humor faded as he eyed her grimly. "I'd have thought you had more sense than to be out on a night like this, but I guess you've proved me wrong."

Brushing a sodden strand of hair from her forehead, she glared back at him. "Does it seem so strange that I'm in a hurry to get home?"

"No . . . not considering that you got a real late start."

Carly winced. He was right, but that didn't make it any easier to hear. "That's not fair. You know nothing about it."

Saying that, she stumbled over a particularly rough spot. Lucas's hand shot out to steady her. He kept hold of her arm as he said quietly, "You'd be surprised what I know. Remember I left too."

The warmth of his touch undermined her instinctive wariness of him. Before she could consider the implications, she murmured, "I was thinking about that, a while ago."

"About me?"

"Don't look so surprised. You hadn't faded entirely from my mind."

"That's reassuring." His dry rejoinder made her laugh despite herself. How like them to meet again for the first time in ten years—and two months—and take up as though they had seen each other only a few days ago. There was no strangeness between them, no uncertainty in the face of long separation.

They were just as they had always been. But what was that exactly? Two people whose instinctive alliance against small-mindedness and prejudice was restrained by a hereditary feud? Two people who might have been friends if not for the ever-present undercurrent of sexual tension that rippled between them?

In the first few moments of being with him again, Carly realized that all the old feelings were still present, only more so. Far from having forgotten anything, she was swept away by a resurgence of emotion so powerful as to unnerve her.

Shivering, she wrapped her arms around herself and tried not to look at him. She might have succeeded, had he not chosen that moment to draw her closer to him. "Come on. We've got to get in out of this."

A rivulet of water inched its way down his lean cheek, shadowed by a day's growth of beard. Droplets caught on the black fringe of his lashes. The wind tugged at his yellow rain slicker and blew up under her fleece jacket to claw at her damp skin.

"My jeep's back there," she said quickly. "If you'll just point me in the right direction, I'll be on my way."

"I don't think so," Lucas muttered. "I'll guide you to your folks' place, but first we need to talk."

Reaching the jeep, he slid in beside her before she could protest. With the doors closed against the storm and the windshield obscured by a sheet of water, they were insulated in a tiny world apart from everything else. The jeep rocked slightly in the wind and they could hear the murmuring protests of tree branches swaying under the onslaught. But otherwise there was only quiet and a solitude that spoke of intimacy.

In the confines of the front seat Carly moved a little away from him. Not that there was really anywhere to go, but she had to at least make the gesture. It was not wasted on Lucas. From some inner pocket of his slicker he pulled a clean handkerchief and handed it to her. "Here, dry yourself off and try to relax a little. I don't much want to spend the next few minutes cooped up with a woman who looks like she thinks I'm about to jump her."

"Then go away," Carly groused. "No one invited you in here."

He laughed, showing white teeth in the darkness. "You always were a scrapper. I'm glad that hasn't changed."

"And you were always arrogant. That's obviously still the same."

"Touché. Now that you've gotten that out of your system, do you think it would be possible for us to have a straightforward conversation about a topic I suspect interests us both?"

Blotting her face with the handkerchief, which had picked up the crisp, cool scent of his body, she eyed him warily. "What's that?"

Lucas nodded toward the backseat and the clutter of boxes and bundles. "If that stuff is anything to go by, you've come back intending to practice medicine here. Correct?"

"Yes, but what's that got to do with you?"

"More than you might think. I came back because I think the people here need all the help they can get, including legal assistance. The coal company has run this valley for too long. It's time for change. Is it fair to say you feel the same way?"

"Yes . . . although I'd be careful who I said that to. We're not the first people to challenge the company. In the past opposition has been stepped on pretty hard."

"That's what I was about to point out to you. I hope you intend to be damn careful about what you do and who you talk to."

"I intend to do my job as a doctor," she told him flatly.

"Talking doesn't come into it. My actions will make my intentions clear."

"Very noble, but would you mind if I inject a note of realism into this? Just how do you plan to get these people to accept you as a doctor?"

"You're not the only one with a handle on the real world, Lucas. I've done my time out there just like you. These people—my people—will accept me when they see that I do my job well."

Was that a gleam of admiration flitting through his cobalt eyes? Carly didn't let herself believe so. To seek his approval would be the first step down a road she was determined not to walk.

She drew her jacket more closely around her as she said, "Look, I'm glad you want to help them too, and I wish you the best of luck. But I don't see how we have anything more to say to each other. You go your way and I'll go mine."

A frown marred the smoothness of his brow beneath tumbled black hair. "We share the same goal of improving life in the Hollow, so why shouldn't we combine forces?"

"You mean . . . work together?"

He grinned wryly. "Don't sound so shocked. That's not exactly an immoral proposition."

"What about our families?"

"I take it you're referring to the ancient and seemingly eternal feud between the Hanlons and the Murdocks?"

"It's nothing to scoff at, Lucas. You know that. There's been bad blood between our families for generations."

"I seem to remember that the two of us managed to get past that on more than one occasion."

"We talked to each other, that's all. And even to do that we had to sneak around, make sure no one knew.

Don't try to tell me that the reason we always met down by the lake was because we happened to like the view. Nobody else ever went there, so it was safe for us."

"And it wouldn't be now?"

"Not the way you're talking about, out in the open and all. Time hasn't changed anything, Lucas. It rarely does in the Hollow."

He leaned back in his seat, looking at her quietly. Light filtering through the sea of drops on the windshield cast the broad planes and hollows of his face into sharp relief. The color of his burnished skin was blanched out. His rough-hewn features might have been carved from a block of white oak, left unfinished by some master craftsman who was content to let time and circumstance put the final stamp on his creation.

"The years have changed you," he said gently. "Ten years ago you were a beautiful, wild thing poised to run at the slightest urging. Now you're lovelier than ever, but strong enough to stay and fight. That's what coming back is all about, isn't it?"

Carly didn't answer him at once. She was too caught up in his description of her as beautiful. Was that really what he thought? She touched her drenched hair and smiled. "You're a flatterer, Lucas. Is that what they teach you in law school?"

His mouth tightened. He shook his head impatiently. "I've no reason to flatter, Carly. If you've been away too long to recognize the truth, I'm sorry for you."

She bit her lip to stop its sudden trembling. How easily he undermined her defenses and made her feel once more a confused young girl, trembling on the brink of womanhood. She yearned to believe he thought her beautiful, even as she told herself such an indulgence had no place in the larger scheme of who she was and what she intended to achieve.

"The truth," she repeated, "is that you're a Murdock and I'm a Hanlon. Our families have been enemies back five generations. When Duncan Murdock got Judith Hanlon with child out of wedlock, then refused to stand up with her, he put an end to the friendship between our kin. There's been nothing but hatred and suspicion since."

"Duncan paid with his life for whatever he'd done," Lucas snapped. "Don't you think that was enough?"

"His death was an accident; it had nothing to do with what happened between him and Judith. Not even all the Murdocks' lies could make that so."

"If he hadn't gone away to fight for the North at Gettysburg, Hanlons would have killed him, and you know that as well as I. He left to prevent bloodshed." Lucas laughed bitterly and then added, "I wonder what old Duncan would make of things now, more than a hundred years later and the feud still in full flower."

His mocking skepticism prompted her to point out what to her at least was obvious. "Listen to us, Lucas. We're talking about Duncan and Judith as though their sorrow happened only a few years ago, instead of more than a century. If the memory is that strong in us, how do you think our families would react to our attempt to work together?"

He rubbed a weary hand along the back of his neck. Watching him, Carly had to restrain herself from reaching out to take over the task. Her fingers itched with the imagined feel of his ebony hair entwined around them.

At length he laid his head back against the seat and said, "I can't deny you have a point. We've a tough enough job to change things in the Hollow without giving anyone an obvious reason to reject our efforts. But damn it, Carly, the feud has to end sometime."

"I thought about this a lot while I was away," she said quietly, not adding that he, more than the feud, had been the unshakable presence in her mind. "The problems between our families are just a symptom of larger problems in the valley. I know your people are far better off than most, including mine, but that's only come about in the last generation after the feud became a fact of life. If your pa had sold his subsoil rights like the rest of them, you'd have no more money than anyone else. Your family's wealth hasn't changed their attitudes. The feud has always been an outlet for anger caused by more complex forces. It remains that way right up to this day."

"I agree, and that's why things have to change. Where we differ is that you seem to think the solution has to start with the big problem, namely the coal company, and I believe we should begin with what's closest to home, ourselves."

"Differences of opinion between Hanlon and Murdock aren't exactly news," Carly reminded him gently. He'd said nothing she really disputed, but neither had he convinced her there was any chance for them to work together without exacerbating an already difficult situation.

They were both silent for several minutes, staring out at the rain, trying to think of some way around their seeming impasse. They both loved their families and were loyal to them, yet they also believed that the feud was wrong and had to end.

"Maybe you're right," Lucas said finally. "Going up against the coal company does seem easier than trying to settle anything between our kin."

"We can still try though. Quietly, without being obtrusive about it. The best thing would be if they just decided for themselves that they'd had enough and made up on their own."

"Do you really think that's likely to happen?" he asked dubiously.

"Yes, I believe that as things start to change for the better in the Hollow, a lot of bitterness will fade."

In the intimacy of the front seat they were almost close enough to be touching. She could feel the damp warmth of his body and smell the fragrance of wood smoke and pine that was an intrinsic part of her memories of him. When Lucas raised a hand to brush it gently along the curve of her chin, one callused finger lingering in the dimpled cleft, she made no effort to draw away.

"I meant what I said about your being beautiful, Carly. Inside as well as out. I'm glad to see you didn't lose that in your time away."

"Trust you to pick this moment to tell me you think that," she murmured shakily. "My feet have gone so cold I can't even feel them, and as for the rest of me . . . I suspect a mud lark would look better."

He moved a little closer to her, his breath warm on her cheek. "I'm sorry you're so cold. I should have got you home right away instead of keeping you talking. We'll go in a moment, but first . . ."

She knew he meant to kiss her. Ten years before beside the lake she'd seen the same fire in his eyes and understood it then. At eighteen she'd been a skittish fawn afraid of his slightest touch. That had changed. Changed utterly.

In place of fear was desire. She wanted him so badly that she ached. There was an emptiness inside her throbbing with the need to be filled. The terrible sense of deprivation that burned through her brought a shock of surprise. She'd never wanted any man with even a fraction of this unbridled, unashamed voluptuousness.

The sheer force of it stunned her. Hers was a reasoned, ordered life in which passion was reserved for the vocation of medicine. There was no room for the reckless wildness of sensual ardor. She had thought herself immune to it, until now.

Was there such a thing as self-willed amnesia? Perhaps, for she seemed to be a victim of it. Remembering him as clearly as she did, how had she managed to forget what he made her feel? The dark, whirling confusion of emotions had been too much for her ten years before. Was it still?

There was only one way to find out. Instinct and a desperate kind of courage drove her to sway toward him, closing the last infinitesimal gap between them until at last, slowly and tentatively, his lips touched hers.

The kiss was gentle, almost as chaste as any they might have shared as children. Yet there was a difference; not a child but a man, full grown and sure of himself, held her. She felt that in his touch, in the utter absence of any need to dominate or enforce his will on her. Only a man sure of what he wanted and his ability to get it could afford to be so tender.

She pressed her body against his, discovering the hard, tensile strength of him. His scent filled her breath even as his warmth engulfed her. Giving in at last to the urge to touch him, she let her hands cup the back of his head, fingers becoming tangled in the thick hair that tapered to the nape of his neck.

Her lips parted on a soundless sigh and the nature of the kiss changed. Lucas hesitated a moment before gently tracing the ridge of her teeth with his tongue, coaxing her to open farther for him until she wanted that more than anything.

So much for the idea that she was now a sophisticated woman of the world. The sweet combat of thrust and parry sent a molten rush of heat through her. She felt the tremor that raced through him and knew she answered in kind.

They clung together, oblivious to the world outside, until at last Lucas raised his head and smiled shakily. "Hell fire, woman, you're enough to make a man forget himself but good." Straightening, he touched a gentle hand to her flushed cheek. "But this isn't the time or place. When it happens between us, I want it to be perfect."

His presumption shattered the cloud of bliss surrounding her. Shaking off his touch, she glared at him. "You overstep yourself. I didn't ask for that."

To her intense annoyance, he smiled, a slow, lazy smile that spoke of assurance she was not as yet experienced enough to share. "Didn't you? Your eyes ask for more than you know. So does your mouth and as for your body . . ."

The sudden fierce blush that swept over her made him laugh. "You can't know how tempted I am to prove what we can share. But much as I hate to admit it, we need to wait until a few other things are sorted out."

About to deny his assertion, she was stopped by the tip of a callused finger pressed lightly against lips still full and moist from his kiss. "Later, Carly. Now that you're home, we have the time we need."

In the dim light filtering through the raindrops, she saw again the fire deep in his eyes in the region where the soul dwells and she knew, in the instinctive way of a woman, what he would say even before the soft words of caution fell between them. "Just don't expect me to be patient too long."

CHAPTER THREE

The house was just as she remembered it: a two-story structure of hand-hewn wood planks recently given a fresh coat of white paint. A porch ran the length of the front, framed on both sides by the spreading arms of old oak trees. The old swing attached by chains to the roof of the porch swayed back and forth, its rhythmic creaking a familiar sound Carly had listened to on many a night such as this.

The original part of the house had been built by her great-great-grandfather when he first came out from Philadelphia seeking land of his own. Succeeding generations had left their own mark, adding on as family size required and rare bursts of prosperity allowed. Some of the newer rooms were set at odd angles, giving the whole an appearance that was at once ramshackle yet sturdy.

Even in the darkness of a rain-splattered night it looked warm and safe. Smoke curled from the big stone chimney. A lamp shone at the kitchen window where paisley curtains had been left opened.

Carly turned the motor off and sat for a moment, letting the sense of home seep slowly over her. Lucas had turned away at the top of the road, coming no farther where he knew he would not be welcomed. She appreciated his tact, even as she regretted the need for it.

A shape moved by the lighted window. The door was flung open. Two figures stood there, one tall and lean, the other smaller and rounder. A voice called on the night air. "Carly . . . that you?"

Ma. She was out of the jeep in an instant, heedless of the rain. Gravel crunched under her feet as she ran the last little distance. Her eyes searched hungrily, drinking in the sight of them.

Her parents were just as she remembered, yet different. A little more gray in her mother's hair swept back in its usual neat bun, a few more wrinkles on her father's lean, weathered face, especially around his clear hazel eyes. But still the same in all the ways that really counted.

Beaming smiles crinkled tear-wet cheeks as she was engulfed in a heartfelt embrace. "Carly . . . welcome home . . ." Seth Hanlon murmured, his deep voice unaccustomedly husky. "Let us look at you," her mother exclaimed. "Land, those photos you sent didn't do you justice! You're prettier than ever."

"Come on now, Rachel. Our girl's wet through. Let's not be standing out in the cold."

"We weren't sure you'd be coming tonight," Ma said as they all made their way inside. "What with the weather so poor, and all. But when we didn't hear anything, we thought you must be on the way. I hope you were careful, child."

"I was, Ma. I just couldn't wait any longer, not being so close."

Her mother squeezed her gently round the waist as her father's hand tightened on hers. "Course you couldn't," he said. "We've been on pins and needles here all day. Your ma's been cookin' anything that would stand still long enough to get in a pot and Timmy here . . ."

"Hi, Sis. Don't look like the big city changed you none." Her youngest brother, with the gentle brown eyes so like their mother's and the unruly shock of sun-streaked hair, hugged her exuberantly, lifting her clear off her feet while she laughed and kissed him soundly on his cheek.

"I swear you've gotten even bigger since I left. Think you'll ever stop growing?"

"Not if Katie keeps feeding me so good." Letting go of her, he held out a hand to his wife of six months, who came forward shyly to meet the sister-in-law spoken of so often yet still a stranger from the wide world beyond.

"Welcome home, Carly," she murmured kindly. "We're right pleased you're back."

"Thank you, Katie. I can see now why this brother of mine was so anxious to get himself hitched."

They all laughed at the young bride's pleased blush as the tall, rangy man who had stood off to one side came forward to claim his turn. "You're a sight for sore eyes, little sister." Older brother, Will, grinned broadly. His hair was the same chestnut hue as Carly's, and his eyes held the same green-gold glints. Though he was three years her senior, they had always been close, and seeing him again added to the deep happiness already overflowing within her.

Swept into his sturdy arms, she was subjected to a rib-crunching hug before he added mischievously, "Yes, sure, you do look good, considering you must have swum here."

"Now leave the girl be," a thin but firm voice insisted. Rising from her chair by the wood stove, Gramma Hanlon leaned on her cane as she surveyed her long-absent granddaughter. She was dressed like the other women in a store-bought blouse and skirt with a homespun shawl over her bent shoulders. Her worn, gentle face creased in a smile that reached all the way to her wise old eyes.

Carly swallowed hard as she went into her grandmother's arms. She could feel the added frailness of her bones worn down by yet another decade on top of all the others that had gone before. Yet there was still great strength, if not of the body then of the spirit. Gramma Hanlon would be ninety soon. She accepted age as gracefully as she did all else that life chose to throw her way.

"I told them you'd be here," she said when at last they stood apart to look at each other. "Told Seth it wouldn't be much longer."

Her father nodded, looking from his mother to his daughter. "She did that, Carly. Even insisted we put the warming pan to your bed in case you wanted to turn in right away."

In her son's house, which had once been her house, Gramma Hanlon was a respected figure. If she said something should be done, it was. Remembering the feel of warmed sheets on a chilly night, Carly smiled. "I appreciate that, but I'm so happy to be home I may not sleep at all tonight. There's so much to catch up on."

Gramma Hanlon laughed appreciatively. "Now what makes you think that, girl? You know nothin' ever happens in the Hollow."

"Then how come we find so much to talk about?" Rachel chided good-humoredly. She smoothed her apron over her neat dress as she surveyed the scene with a satisfied smile. The family was complete again. Her missing fledgling, flown from the nest, was home.

"You may not be tired, Carly, but I'll bet you could put away some food. Didn't they feed you in the city?"

Arm in arm with Will and Timmy, she followed the rest of her family to the kitchen. "Sure they did, Ma. The hospital cafeteria was famous for its canned green beans, white bread, and meat loaf."

Her mother's face paled. Bustling over to the big cast-iron stove, she took the lid off a pot and stirred it vigorously. Delectable smells rose in a cloud of steam. "You sit yourself down right now, child. We're going to get some decent food in you before it's too late."

Decent did not quite begin to describe the feast laid before her. There were all the favorite foods of her childhood: venison stew flavored with onions, potatoes, peas, and dill seeds from her mother's garden, crusty whole-wheat bread sweetened with honey, gingered peaches put up in summer, apple-cranberry pie topped with fresh churned vanilla ice cream, all washed down by cold milk from their own cows or coffee strong enough to stand a spoon up in.

While they ate, they talked. "I wish we could tell you things are better in the Hollow," Pa said. "But the plain truth is that not much has changed. The government people try, but all the welfare in the world is not going to help what's wrong here."

"You still of the same mind about the problem, Pa?" Carly asked.

He nodded firmly. "Too much power in the hands of too few people. Those men who run the coal company just don't care about folks here. They're too far away, with no stake in the community."

"The blame isn't all theirs," Willy said quietly. "Folks here made the mistake of selling mineral rights out from under ourselves. I know that was back during the Depression when people needed money real bad, but it sure was a shame they didn't figure what it would lead to."

"It's hard to think that far ahead when you're worryin' about puttin' food on the table for your children," Gramma pointed out. "Only person who refused to go along with the company owners was old man Murdock, and his kids suffered for it. I admit they've got it good now, but are you sayin' you wish the rest of us were like them?"

"No," Willy admitted. "I don't have no fondness for Murdocks. But you got to give them credit for being smart."

"Smart and mean," Timmy chimed in. "I hear Lucas is back. Word is he plans to take on the coal company by hisself if he has to."

Pa snorted and poured himself another cup of coffee. "They deserve each other. Murdocks are trouble."

"Why, Pa?"

The words were out before she could stop them. In the sudden silence that descended on the table, Carly breathed in sharply. It was bad enough that she had at last given voice to the question that should never have been asked, but to do so on the night of her homecoming . . .

" 'Pears you've been away longer than we thought, Carly," Will murmured finally.

As criticism went, it wasn't much. But considering the source, the chiding was painful. Her throat tightened as she looked round at the suddenly somber faces of her kin. Their approval was precious to her, but not so much that she would sacrifice her belief in what was right.

"Before I left here," she said quietly, "I thought the feud was wrong. I didn't say so at the time because I was only eighteen and it wasn't my place to speak out like that. But I think you all suspected how I felt. Nothing I learned in college or afterward changed my mind about that. I can understand disliking an individual, but not a whole group of people just because of who they happen to be."

The Hanlons looked around at each other in the speaking way families have. Then attention focused back down on their plates. There was silence again for several moments before Rachel said softly, "Aren't you forgetting that the Murdocks have done us injury?"

"*A* Murdock injured *a* Hanlon more than a hundred years ago. How much longer are we going to let that have such a strong hold over our lives?"

"You talk like nothing's happened since then," Willy said. "We've had trouble with the Murdocks straight through, arguments about the boundaries of our lands, pasture rights, all sorts of things."

"Only because both they and us were determined not to get along. Neighbors should have been able to settle those problems peaceably."

"Maybe so, Carly," Pa said. "But what ought to be and what is are often two different things. The Murdocks don't trust us any more than we trust them."

Much as she wished she could deny it, that was true. The situation was a stalemate, with neither side willing to make the first move. So it had been for generations, and so it looked to remain. Unless she and Lucas could reach some private accord that would prompt their families to relent. That was what he had suggested back on the road, and what she had rejected because of the disloyalty it entailed.

Yet was it disloyalty to do what you truly believed was right for all concerned? She pondered that as the meal concluded and the women began washing up. Standing at the sink between her mother and sister-in-law, she dried dishes and joined in their talk automatically. The larger part of her mind was focused squarely on the problem of what, if anything, she could do to bring about the reconciliation both she and Lucas wanted.

If she were going to attempt that at the risk of losing her family's respect, then she had to be sure there was some chance of success. For all the warmth of their welcome, she was still partly a stranger to them. They would be watching her to see what changes the years and the outside world had wrought. And their scrutiny would be nothing compared to that of the rest of the Hollow people, who would regard with suspicion someone who had dared to venture out into the larger world.

First she had to win her way back into her family's and the community's trust. Then she could set about the process of finding some end to the feud that drew vital attention from the abuses of the coal company.

A sigh escaped her as she thought about how unnecessary it all was. If only people were able to forget the past and go on . . . But they weren't, any more than she was. The past, good and bad, was a precious legacy. In its intricate twists and turns were signposts pointing the way to a better future.

To become all that she knew she could be, she had to keep a hold of all she had been. It wasn't easy but she thought she had at last struck some sort of balance between the two. Coming home was her way of finding out if she was right.

Much later after the family had at last drifted off to find its rest, she lay in bed in her room under the eaves, listening to the chiming of the clock on the stairway landing and thinking about the bittersweet pain of homecoming.

Though the night was chill and damp, she was snug under a pile of quilts. Rain splattered against the small round window, which as a child she had pretended was the porthole of a vessel traveling across a great sea. The branches of the oak just beyond had been the masts; she'd sat in them many times dreaming of the great world outside the Hollow.

Having gone there, faced the challenges, and done all she had hoped to, she would have thought her dreams fulfilled. Yet she was discovering they remained as shining and elusive as ever. Only now she could see, as before she could not, that it wasn't the outside world that held the key to all she wanted, but the inner world of her heritage.

She was of the Hollow; nothing could change that. It was time to make her peace with the place and with the man who more than any other represented all she had turned away from and all she was at last ready to confront.

Far off in a secret corner of her heart she heard the cry of the mountain hawk seeking its mate and knew again the tremulous flutter of wings beating to be free.

CHAPTER FOUR

Carly went into town early the next morning, intending to scout out a storefront or other suitable setting to open her practice. Will and Timmy went along with a list of supplies needed for the house and farm. They parted on the main street near Pearson's General Store.

"I'll meet you back here in a bit," Carly said. "Okay?"

Her brothers nodded and grinned. "Sure thing, honey," Timmy said. "What with Ma's list and Pa's list and Gramma's list and Katie's list, we'll be a while."

Will laughed, nudging his brother toward the door. "Take your time, Sis. There's a couple of empty stores down toward the creek. Might find something there to suit you."

As they disappeared into the shadowy interior, Carly turned in the direction Will had indicated. She stood for a moment surveying the single business street that comprised the town of Spruce Hollow.

Directly across from Pearson's General Store was the old Luxor Movie Theater where she had spent many a Saturday afternoon perched on a scratchy velveteen chair chewing stale popcorn and watching magical images flicker across the cracked and stained screen.

Next to it was the Modern Luncheonette, something of a misnomer since it appeared to have been lifted intact out of the late 1940s, when, in fact, it had been built.

A favorite stopover for miners on their way to and from work, as well as farmers in town to shop, the luncheonette did a brisk business in thick egg sandwiches, wedges of lemon meringue pie, and coffee that puckered the tongue.

Farther down the street was Maybelle Lane's Beauty Parlor, six dryers no waiting. Accustomed to the unisex haircutting salons of the big city, Carly was tempted to smile at the thought of women sitting patiently in pink plastic curlers until it came their turn to be brushed, teased, and lacquered.

But she remembered afternoons there with her mother, sitting on the floor listening to the slow, matter-of-fact talk of birth and death, love and pain. That was the first place she had begun to sense what it was to be a woman.

The other side of the street was rounded out by a gas station, bank, and the VFW hall. Together with Pearson's General Store, which sold everything from bailing wire to toothpaste and also housed the post office, they took care of all the community's immediate needs.

For anything else residents drove to Branchville, or if they were after something really special and were willing to make a day of it, into Parkersburg.

From time to time, as brief spates of prosperity moved across the coal hills, other stores opened. Few remained long. As Will had said, there were a number of vacant buildings that looked worth considering.

Peering through the grime-encrusted window of one, Carly saw the remnants of what had briefly been a newsstand and video game parlor. It wasn't hard to figure what had gone wrong.

People thereabouts didn't take kindly to children wasting time and money at such foolishness, nor did they care for the "girlie" magazines the store had carried. There was a wide streak of prudery running through the Hollow, an interesting counterpoint to the high rate of early marriages and large families.

Without going inside the store, it was hard to tell much about its potential. But the location was good and it looked large enough. Making a mental note to check at the bank, which kept track of local real estate, Carly started on back down the street.

About halfway back to the General Store, she became aware of the three women watching her. They had just left Maybelle Lane's and were pausing a moment to give the town the full benefit of their new hairdos before starting on home. The small children they had in tow tugged at them impatiently, only to break off when they, too, became abruptly aware of Carly.

The women glanced at her in the quick, darting way of people shy about strangers. The children were less abashed. They stared openly as she crossed the street to join the group.

" 'Morning, Hester . . . Philona . . . Emily. It's nice to see you all again."

Pleased smiles all around as her initiative erased their hesitation. Carly, too, smiled as she wondered how they had expected her to act with people she had known all her life—stuck up and holier than thou?

"Well . . . now . . . isn't this a nice surprise," Hester said. She had always been inclined to take the lead, with the others' full consent. Carly had a mental image of her as a high school cheerleader, vibrant and exuberant with well-scrubbed good looks. Ten years had dimmed the light in her eyes and thickened her waist, but otherwise hadn't changed her too much.

"Welcome home, Carly. We heard you were comin'."

"Thank you, Hester. It's good to be here." Glancing down at the wide-eyed children, she added, "Let's see now if I can guess which of these is yours . . . This one, right?" Her hand touched the bright red hair of a little boy about six years old.

The other women chuckled as Hester nodded proudly. "I'll plead guilty to that, but how did you know?"

"Simple, he's got Davy Willis's carrot top, and there was never any question but that the two of you would make a couple."

"We did, indeed, right after graduation. Got two more at home." She looked at Carly assessingly, taking in the fitted jeans, soft plaid shirt, and moss-green sweater that complemented her slender figure. "Doesn't seem possible ten years could go by so fast."

"That's the truth. Now who do the rest of these belong to?"

"These two are mine," Philona said, indicating a boy and girl, both under five. The little girl hid against her mother's skirt, peering out with one eye. Her brother was a little braver. He faced the stranger stalwartly, but kept a tight grip on his mother's hand.

Carly remembered Philona as an angelic blond girl who had once confided in her that she also dreamed of leaving the Hollow. She might have done it too, if not for Walt Millard, quarterback of the high school football team, who had persuaded her to go just a little farther than maybe she should have and gotten her with child.

They had married right after graduation, when there was always a spate of weddings, with Philona wearing a high-waisted dress to conceal the pregnancy everybody already knew about anyway.

"The rest of 'em are in school right now," she added with a wan smile. "Thank the Lord for small mercies."

Carly laughed and bent down to smile at the last of the children, a baby in a stroller. "Yours, Emily?"

The shy dark-haired young woman flushed prettily. In a soft, breathy voice, she murmured, "This is Adeline. She's my first." The mother's eyes rested on her child with a glimmer of awe, as though she could still hardly believe in the miracle so long despaired of but at last come into her life.

"She's beautiful," Carly said sincerely. "You should be very proud."

Emily smiled gratefully. "We really are glad to have you back. Are you going to stay?"

"Yes, I'm going to practice medicine here."

There was a moment's silence before Hester murmured, "So it's true what we heard. You're a doctor?"

"I'd better be, or they gave me that license for nothing."

The women laughed, but guardedly. There was a new wariness in their eyes that came not from the fear of disdain but from the encounter with something completely outside their experience.

"A doctor," Emily said at last. "Imagine that."

"We've already got a doctor," Philona pointed out, not unkindly. "In Branchville."

"That's twenty miles from here," Carly said quietly. "Over rough roads. I thought it would be better if people in the Hollow had a doctor of their own."

Silence again, until Hester broke it. "Well, now . . . maybe there's something to that. But still . . . a woman doctor."

"I know it's a surprise, but I am good at what I do. All I ask is a chance to show you that."

They thought about that for a moment until Philona asked, "So many places you could have gone, what made you come back here?"

A fair question, but still tough to answer in a way these proud people could accept. Carefully, Carly said, "This is my home. There's nowhere else I want to be."

That was the truth and deserved to be respected as such, but would they realize that? Skepticism was understandable, given her long absence.

"That's good to hear," Philona ventured. "We all think the Hollow is special, but then most of us haven't been away."

Carly nodded, recognizing the tentative leaning toward, if not acceptance, then at least tolerance. "Sometimes you have to go away to get the right perspective on a place. If I'd stayed here, I'd have been plagued by dreams of leaving, and they would have prevented me from seeing all I had. As it is, I've come back not just prepared to stay, but determined."

Hester smiled slightly at this. She had always admired courage. "That's good, Carly. It'll take determination to convince some folks here to accept a woman doctor."

"I know that, and I'm not asking for any concessions. You have a right to expect the best possible medical care. That's what I aim to provide."

They glanced at each other, not wanting to be impolite but also unwilling to commit themselves before they saw the general drift of things. "We wish you the best," Emily offered gently. She darted a quick look at her friends before she added, "When you're settled, I'll drop by to say hello."

Carly nodded, appreciating the implication of that.

"Thank you. I hope you'll all come by, and feel free to bring your children. I know a lot of them are afraid of doctors' offices, but I'm going to try to change that."

The women smiled, still uncertain. They drifted off a few minutes later, heads bent in conversation. Carly watched them go with mixed feelings. The ice had certainly been broken, but she had no illusions of having accomplished anything more than a first, tentative step. Much more would have to happen before they would trust her enough to accept the changes she represented.

Coming out of the bank a short time later, she stood on the street to collect her thoughts and let the sun warm her face. Banker Davies had been encouraging up to a point.

Yes, the storefront was available and within her budget. But beyond that, he made no bones about the fact that he thought she was wrong to try to set up a medical practice in Spruce Hollow.

"There's no need for what you've got in mind, Carly." Leaning back in his big chair, he arranged his florid face solemnly. Thin sandy hair in the process of turning gray clung to his bullet-shaped head. He wore a nondescript brown suit and white shirt with a knit tie. Of medium height and build, he was carrying about forty pounds more than he should have; a great deal of it settled around his straining middle.

The jowls of his cheeks quivered slightly as he added, "Folks here have all the medical care they need. Old Dr. Falkston over at Branchville does a fine job, and there's a tip-top first-aid station at the mines."

Listening to him, she took a deep breath, determined not to let her irritation show. Floyd Davies had the self-righteous air of a man who has chosen to believe he genuinely merits the privileges conferred on him by an accident of birth.

His father had run the bank before him, working hand in glove with the coal company to their mutual benefit. Spruce Hollow and its people were very low on his list of priorities, if they appeared on it at all. He was concerned only with maintaining the status quo that served him and a few others so well.

Carly had anticipated his objections to her plans and set out to disarm them. "I know there's been a lot of talk lately about the coal company owing more to the people, Floyd. But frankly I'm a little surprised to discover that you think that way."

His small pale blue eyes widened slightly. "What do you mean? I didn't say that."

"What was that about the first-aid station then? I thought it was only supposed to be available in case of an accident at the mines. But if townspeople can rely on it for their ordinary medical care . . ."

"Carly Hanlon, you're twisting my words and you know it. Doc Falkston takes care of folks' regular needs."

"Not twenty miles away in Branchville, he doesn't," she said, letting a little of the steel slip into her voice. "Nobody goes to him unless they have absolutely no alternative, and by then the damage is so severe he generally can't help. That's not my idea of adequate medical care."

Sticking the stub of a cold cigar in his mouth, Floyd Davies frowned at her. "Do I have to remind you that your ideas come from the big city? What makes you think they'll be accepted by folks hereabouts?"

"I don't know for sure that they will be," she admitted candidly. "But I aim to try, even if I have to pitch a tent."

Sensing that she had pushed him far enough, she leaned back in her chair and gave him a conciliatory smile. "What have you got to lose by renting me the property? It's just sitting there now not earning a cent. If I fail, you'll at least get a few months' income out of it. And if I succeed, you'll be assured of a steady profit. Either way, the townspeople will feel you tried to do something for them and they'll respect you for it. Seems to me it's just good business to accept a proposition like mine."

He chewed that over for a while, sucking on the cigar and studying her. Carly met his scrutiny calmly. She knew he was trying to rile her, to unearth some sign of weakness that would mean she didn't really have to be taken seriously. But she gave him none.

At length he shrugged, saving face by pretending it wasn't all that important. "Tell you what, you put up six months' rent as security and you've got a deal."

The smug tilt of his pursed mouth told her he didn't think she had the money. But Carly hadn't pinched pennies for ten years for nothing. She smiled warmly and nodded. "If you'll have the lease drawn up for my inspection, I'll write you a check."

Banker Davies frowned. He hadn't expected that. "Check? Well, now, if it's drawn on some out-of-state bank, that'll take a while to process."

"I moved my funds to Parkersburg before coming back here. You won't need more than a couple of days to verify that the check is good. In the meantime, I expect the lease to be processed. As I'm sure you understand, I'm anxious to get started."

Rising before he could object, she held out a hand to him. "It's a pleasure doing business with you, Floyd. I'm sure we'll deal well together."

He rose automatically and shook hands, but not without a frustrated scowl that suggested he knew he was trapped and didn't like it. Carly didn't mind. She accepted that Banker Davies would spend the next few days trying to maneuver out of the deal.

Eventually he would convince himself he had nothing to worry about because she couldn't, despite what she claimed, come up with either the money or the determination to see the venture through. And he would be wrong.

Back out on the sidewalk she breathed deeply. The first major hurdle was passed. Many more remained, but at least she was on her way. The urge to tell Timmy and Will surged through her and sent her hurrying down the street toward Pearson's.

But before she could get there, an all too familiar pickup truck pulled up beside her, and Lucas got out, easing his big body from behind the wheel with unconscious grace.

"Morning, Carly," he said, letting his eyes run over her in the caressing way she both loved and hated. "Looks like you're getting an early start."

She nodded warily, fighting the wave of pleasure that washed over her at the mere sight of him. The jeans and workshirt he wore should have looked perfectly ordinary, but on him they were inordinately attractive.

She was acutely aware of his broad shoulders and muscular chest, of the tapered line of his waist and hips, and of the powerful legs planted slightly apart in a stance that was at once aggressive and confident.

"Lucas, nice to see you. Get home all right last night?"

He came away from the side of the truck, walking toward her slowly, his pure blue gaze never flickering. "Oh, yes, though Pa and my brothers were a little puzzled about why I'd been gone so long." He smiled as if he were drawing her into a private world all their own.

Trying to resist his appeal, she took a step back. "What did you tell them?"

He frowned slightly, covering the distance between them until he was standing directly in front of her. "The truth. That you were back and had run into a spot of trouble on the road."

Carly laughed shortly, unable to keep the nervous quiver from her voice. "They must have liked that."

He shrugged in dimissal. "Doesn't matter whether they did or not. I don't share their feelings."

She knew what he was telling her; that she, too, could be as independent, that they could find their own way free of everyone else. Part of her wanted to believe him, but another, stronger part felt the tug of responsibility, reminding her of all she owed to these people and all she had promised herself she would do for them.

To begin by turning her back on one of her family's most closely held beliefs would hardly be a good way to start.

Faced with such a challenge, silence seemed the wisest course. She maintained it long enough for Lucas to become convinced she was not open to persuasion, at least that day. A slight smile curved his mouth as he nodded toward the bank. "Been in to see Floyd?"

That was safer ground. Relieved, she laughed. "Yes, and frankly I think I wrecked his day."

Lucas laughed, a deep, warm sound she found impossible to resent. "Too bad. It won't do him any harm to get shaken up a bit."

"More than a bit," Carly admitted ruefully. "I found a place to set up practice. He doesn't think it's a good idea, but he can't find any way to talk me out of it."

"You always were stubborn. Shouldn't come as a surprise to anyone." The glance he shot her was full of fondness and something else too. There was intimacy in the eyes that held so many memories of her as a little girl, awkward adolescent, budding woman.

Lucas had known her in all those incarnations. Now he was making a bid to discover what she had become and, perhaps, to play a decisive role in shaping what she was to be.

A few years ago, when she was fighting the battle for independence and success, she would have bitterly rejected the suggestion that any man—and especially this one in particular—could play such a decisive role in her life. Now it surprised her that she was able to accept the possibility with such calmness.

His compelling masculinity no longer threatened her; rather, she welcomed it as the natural complement to her womanhood. Were circumstances different, she would not have hesitated to let their relationship develop along what were clearly inevitable lines.

But there were other considerations, despite Lucas's effort to pretend otherwise. Already she was aware of passersby staring at them. The sight of a Hanlon and a Murdock engaged in conversation on the main street of Spruce Hollow was startling enough to break through the citizenry's usual reserve.

A curtain fluttered at the window of Maybelle Lane's; a passing truck slowed to a crawl; several men stuck their heads out of the Modern Luncheonette and pretended to take the air.

Lucas missed none of it. Grinning, he said, " 'Pears as though we're causing quite a stir."

"It's not funny. We'll both hear about this from our families."

His smile vanished, replaced by a frown. "I could understand your being concerned about that back when you were eighteen, but not now. You're an adult, Carly, free to make your own choices."

His exasperation stung her, prompting a sharp retort. "You don't have to tell me what I am, Lucas Murdock. I'm well aware of it. I didn't get where I am today by losing sight of my goals, or by being swayed by the words and beliefs of others."

"Is that what you think this all is, pretty words?"

"What else? You want me to do something I'm against." Throwing caution to the winds, she added, "And we both know working together is just the start of it."

She expected him to deny it, but instead he merely shrugged. "What's wrong with that? You're a beautiful woman with fire in your spirit. I had a powerful yen for you when we were both kids. Over the years it's only grown stronger."

His candor took her aback. She was accustomed to men who were more cautious in their approaches lest they risk rejection. The ritualistic mating dance of men and women, with its elaborate feints and parries, had always amused her.

She had felt above the fray, immune from such distractions. But Lucas's potent brand of attraction cut straight through her defenses to the heart of the matter; she desired him as much as he did her. A flush warmed her cheeks as she contemplated that truth.

"Penny for them," he drawled, the smile firmly back in place and reaching all the way to the eyes that watched her knowingly.

"Never mind. I've got to be going."

"Coward," he taunted softly.

Her head came up, meeting his gaze defiantly. "The word is realist." More gently, she added, "We have to have priorities, Lucas. What comes first, us or the town? I think we both know the answer to that."

He was silent for a moment before nodding reluctantly. There was a new element in his gaze. Grudging respect? He made one last try. "I still claim we would accomplish more if we worked together."

"And I say that's impossible, at least for the moment." She knew she was leaving a door open, something she might later regret, but she couldn't stop herself. Not when every part of her was crying out to take what he was offering.

She had to get away, to recover her composure and remember why she had come so far to fulfill a dream that was also a duty. In the small town it was impossible to steer clear of Lucas. They would see each other often. But at least she could take refuge in her mind and in the images of what was to be that had sustained her through all the difficult years.

"When I get my practice set up," she murmured, "I hope you'll stop by." Let him come onto her own turf and see her as the competent professional that she was. Perhaps that would diminish the ardor of this man who undoubtedly demanded the epitome of femininity in his women.

There was nothing in his attitude to suggest that was the case. Instead he nodded. "I'll look forward to it." Turning back to his truck, he glanced over his shoulder at her. The sudden reappearance of his grin sent a swift wave of apprehension through her.

Sliding behind the wheel, he said, "Maybe we can get together for a cup of coffee or something. After all, neighbors ought to be friendly."

Something warned her he wasn't referring to the common march of their family's lands. Hardly daring to look at him, yet unwilling to do otherwise, she croaked, "Neighbors?"

"Why sure. Didn't Banker Davies tell you? I rented the place next to yours to use as my law office."

With that parting shot he was gone, leaving her to contemplate the folly of her own pleasure at the knowledge that he would be so near.

CHAPTER FIVE

"Where do you want these boxes, Carly?" Will asked as he stumbled through the door with his arms full.

"In the back away from where we'll be working. We've got to get this place scrubbed down before I can start unpacking."

Timmy grinned as he dumped a pile of mops, brooms, and buckets in the center of the room. "Gram would have a fit if she saw this. She thinks a few little dust kittens are shameful."

Carly nodded, pressing a hand to the back of her neck in a futile effort to ease the muscle cramping. They had arrived barely half an hour ago to begin readying the store, and already she was wondering how they would be able to make any headway against the all-pervasive filth and grime.

"Banker Davies did warn me it was in pretty bad shape, and I saw that for myself when I looked the property over before signing the lease. But seeing it is different from actually wading into it."

"I'll say," Will agreed. "But don't worry, Sis. We won't let it get the better of us."

She smiled at him gratefully, well aware that by coming to help her both he and Timmy were missing a day's work on the small family farm. Between all the chores that had to be done there and their regular jobs at the mine, they had little time for anything else. Yet they were giving her precious hours they could ill afford.

Glancing around at the stained floor covered by peeling linoleum and the cracked walls, she sighed inwardly. The bright smile she managed belied her gloomy thoughts about how long it would take to make the place habitable. "Let's get started then. I guess the floor is first."

An hour later, they had made considerable progress in ripping up the linoleum and stacking it in the alley behind the store. The wood floor beneath it was dark with age, but looked sturdy enough. Carly went down the street to Pearson's to see about renting a sander. Her luck was in. It turned out one was available immediately. Leaving a deposit for its return, she set off back to the store. By the time she got there lugging the machine, Katie had just arrived with refreshments.

"You shouldn't be toting that by yourself," her sister-in-law admonished gently. "What're Timmy and Will thinking of?"

"They didn't know I'd be bringing it back," Carly explained. She glanced at the picnic basket Katie was carrying. "I hope that's got some lemonade in it. We're all parched."

Stepping into the store, Katie gave her husband a shy peck on the cheek before finding a clear spot to unpack what looked like lunch for a dozen. "Lemonade . . . brownies . . . fried chicken . . . biscuits . . . and . . ."

—she pulled out a final container—"some of Gramma's special three-bean salad."

"Well, now," Will said, dusting off his hands, "I'd say that looks like decent provisions for hardworkin' folks."

"Only one problem," Timmy pointed out. "If we eat all that we won't be able to move."

"I don't know about you," Carly said, "but I sure don't intend to let it go to waste. Let's get the floor done, then take a break."

As Will and Timmy tackled the sander, Katie joined Carly in stripping old paper from the walls. By noon, they had at least the beginnings of a clean, spacious area awaiting only a fresh coat of paint and some furnishings.

Leaving the front and back doors open to air the place out, they piled into the pickup truck and drove down to the creek for an impromptu picnic. The crisp fall day was pleasantly cool. Dry leaves rustled beneath their feet and squirrels scampered overhead.

The food was delicious, the conversation light and teasing. It reminded Carly of many other such afternoons in her childhood when the whole family gathered to harvest the crops, then enjoyed the fruits of its labors.

As they sat back around the table, relaxing briefly before returning to work, she regarded them fondly. Her years away were not the barrier she had feared. Their acceptance of her as she was now was as warm and loving as she could ever have hoped.

But their acceptance of other things left a great deal to be desired.

"I hear Lucas Murdock was in town the other day," Will said. "Seems he's planning to open a law office."

"Bully for him," Timmy muttered. "What does he think this is, Boston . . . or maybe New York?"

"He'll be mighty disappointed when he finds out folks

round here don't have any use for a lawyer," Katie pointed out.

Carly knew she should hold her tongue, or better yet agree with them. But she couldn't bring herself to do either. Cautiously, she ventured, "I'm not sure that's the case. It seems to me a good lawyer who really cares about people could help deal with the coal company."

"You'll get no argument from me on that," Will said, "but we're talking about Lucas Murdock. What does he care about helpin' people?"

"If he didn't care, why would he come back?"

Tim shrugged. "Who can figure Murdocks?"

Despite herself, Carly grinned. "You know what, I'll bet the whole kit and caboodle of them are sitting around saying the same thing about us."

Her brothers and sister-in-law stared at her for a moment before they, too, smiled reluctantly. "Maybe so," Will allowed. "I wouldn't put anything past that bunch."

They talked awhile longer before Carly glanced at her watch. "Much as I hate to say this, we'd better be getting back."

With a chorus of groans, they rose and cleared away the remnants of the picnic. The autumn sun was lowering westward and a pale crescent moon floated in the sky when they returned to the store. It looked just as they had left it an hour before—both doors standing open to the air and a breeze ruffling the curtains Katie had made for the window.

Carly was the first to realize what had changed; someone was moving around inside. She held her breath, willing the tall, all-too-familiar figure to vanish before anyone else noticed. Her prayer died in the passage of a heartbeat.

"What the hell . . . ?" Timmy growled, taking a step

forward. His wide shoulders blocked the doorway as he confronted the man inside. "Murdock! You've got a damn nerve coming in here."

Lucas turned with apparent unconcern, his gaze settling briefly on Carly before it took in the angry faces of her brothers and Katie's condemning stare. A slight smile touched his mouth. "Just neighborly curiosity, Tim. Or didn't Carly tell you my law office is right next door?"

Perhaps it was the unexpected use of his name or the other man's quiet confidence, but Tim didn't catch the last part of what he had said before taking a step forward, his cheeks flushed and his hands clenched at his sides. "Neighborly? That's a laugh. Get out of here, Murdock, before we—" He broke off for an instant, surprise momentarily washing away anger. "What do you mean, next door?"

"Pretty obvious, isn't it?" Will broke in. He was as irate as his younger brother, but marginally more in control. Still Carly was afraid of just how far they would go, especially since Lucas seemed bent on provoking them.

Shooting him a glance that would have withered a lesser man, she said, "Let's put a stop to this right now. Lucas didn't do anything wrong coming in here. We left the place unlocked, and besides in a few days I hope everyone will share his curiosity and want to see what I'm up to. As for the rest of it, we're not going to settle anything here, so let's just forget it."

"Forget it?" Timmy exclaimed. "You're going to be working next to a Murdock, probably running into him everyday, and you tell us just to *forget* it?"

Vexed at the position Lucas had put her in by his abrupt announcement and still worried about settling the confrontation peacefully, Carly snapped, "That's exactly what I'm telling you. We'd better get something straight, I haven't worked as hard as I did the last few years to be told what to do by any man, Hanlon or Murdock. I'm here for only one reason, to practice medicine. And no one"—she glanced from her brothers to Lucas—"not kin or foe is going to stop me."

In the silence that followed her spirited declaration, Carly could feel her heart beating painfully, and not strictly for reasons that had to do with the feud or any unpleasantness that might arise from it.

Just being so close to Lucas, with only a few yards separating them, was enough to send a wave of warmth surging through her. In the presence of her family yet! She flushed as she considered what would have happened if she had come upon him alone.

Her feelings were complicated by the fact that Lucas was gazing at her with unfeigned admiration. Even her brothers and Katie were grudgingly respectful, though with an undertone of incredulity. They had not expected her to respond quite so vigorously.

"You're a grown woman, Carly," Will murmured at last. "You can do anything you please. But I advise you to remember you'll always be one of us. No amount of wishing—or big-city gloss—can change that."

"I wouldn't want to change it," she said softly, her voice shaking slightly. "I love you all, but that doesn't mean I can share all your beliefs."

It was an old story, she thought, as she watched them look at each other in sad bewilderment. Tolerance was in short supply in the valley. People clung to the idea that you were either for them or against them. Middle ground was not respected, or even acknowledged.

Hardly aware of what she was doing, she looked at Lucas, her hazel eyes holding an entreaty he had neither wish nor will to resist. Taking a deep breath, he went to stand beside her.

In tones that could only be called conciliatory, he said, "Look, I think you should know that I've already asked Carly to work with me and she refused, because she didn't want to upset you. I still think we can be more effective together, but I understand her decision. I'm not about to try to force anything on anyone, not Carly, or you, or the rest of this town. I'm just here to help."

Coming from so proud a man, the admission of his own limitations was deeply moving. At least to Carly. Her brothers looked unaffected, though she thought she saw some flicker of surprise in their taut expressions.

A moment later she realized that was not a good sign. "You asked her?" Will repeated angrily. "Just when did you get the chance to do that?"

Before Lucas could respond, Carly stepped in. The last thing she wanted was trouble, but she wasn't about to let anyone suggest she wasn't free to see and speak with anyone she chose. "I met Lucas the evening I came home and again yesterday. What we said is nobody's business but our own. He's told you the truth, and I'd thank you to accept it."

Will was not accustomed to hearing her speak so sharply. Always before with her family she had been, if not deferential, then at least tactful. But then she had also been very much a child. Now she was anything but a child, and it did not occur to her to pretend otherwise. Yet still the surprise, and the hurt, in her brothers' eyes made her ache inside.

Timmy shoved his hands into the pockets of his jeans. He held himself stiffly, as though braced for a blow. "Does that mean you don't think we should be concerned about who you go with, and what harm they might do you?"

Behind the question was all the traditional protectiveness of the mountain men, who expected their women to submit to their authority and, in return, be sheltered by it. Carly knew that in her brother's case, the expectation sprang at least in part from genuine love. But that didn't make it any easier to tolerate.

Gently, she said, "We all care about each other and watch out for each other. But in this case there's nothing for you to be worried about."

"I don't think Ma and Pa will agree with you," Will murmured. "Much less Gram."

"There's nothing for them to disagree with," Lucas insisted quietly. "I told you, she refused to join forces with me."

Carly nodded, even though she already regretted that decision. It didn't seem to have had the effect she'd hoped. Her family was still upset and she had gained nothing. "But that doesn't mean we won't be civil to each other, or talk over problems. Lucas and I have the same goal, helping the people here. We'll do what's necessary to achieve that."

Will shook his head in bewilderment. "You're both so sure of yourselves, so positive that we want to change. Maybe that's not the case."

"You can't believe that," Carly said softly. "There's a lot in the Hollow that's good—strength, values, courage. No one wants to change that. But there's also a darker side. Poverty, disease, superstition, have to yield to a better way of life."

Her brother's only response was a bewildered look, which Timmy matched. In the strained silence that followed, Katie spoke gently. "We do understand what you're saying, Carly. But are you sure it's possible to cure what ails us without also striking at the very bedrock of our world?"

No, she wasn't sure, though she was loath to admit it. Everything she believed, every ounce of hope she possessed, proclaimed that progress was possible, things could get better. Yet how often had advancement been at the cost of traditional values? How often had a people been wrenched into the present only by the destruction of their past?

If that happened in the Hollow, it would be a tragedy she wanted no part of. Nor, she was certain, did Lucas.

He, at least, had an answer for Katie. "If we were outsiders, you would be right to be leery of us. We've all seen the government people who, well meaning though they are, have no idea how to deal with us. In their ignorance they can do more harm than good. That's not the case with Carly and me. We love the Hollow and its ways. All we want is to build on what we've already got to make things better."

It was an invitation few could have resisted, except those blinded by ancient hatreds and long-held grudges. Will snorted derisively. "Fine words from a Murdock. We always said any of you could charm the birds right out of the trees." His hard gaze flickered over at Carly. "I just hope my sister's got a little more sense than your average barn owl."

"That's not fair, Will," she shot back, unaware that in her distress she had taken a step closer to Lucas. He turned slightly, shielding her with his nearness.

"Lay off her, Hanlon. You're damn lucky to have a sister like her. She's better than any ten other people you could mention put together, and she's got more guts than any of you."

The low growl would have been warning enough even without the aggressive stance of his body, but Will chose not to heed it. The two big, angry men faced each other challengingly. They were almost the same height, Lucas having the advantage by a scant inch. Their builds were similar, hard and lean with a toughness that was more than physical. Both were accustomed to being in control, and neither was about to relinquish rights to the other.

"My sister doesn't need your help," Will grated. "No Hanlon does. We take care of our own."

"You do a real good job of it," Lucas drawled sarcastically. "All Carly wants to do is help people and you're making things tough on her."

"Don't tell me what I'm doing . . ."

"Why not? Can't you take the truth?"

"Why you—"

"Will! Lucas! Stop it right now. I don't need either of you to protect me. I've made my own way for ten years, and I plan to continue doing just that now. So both of you come down off your high horses and kindly remove your noses from my business!"

"Now, Sis, you don't mean that . . ."

"Calm down, Carly. We'll handle this."

"You will? The only way you two know to handle anything is to fight over it. No thanks! Lucas, I appreciate your stopping by, but I think you'd best leave now. Will, I'm glad of your help along with the rest of the family's, but I won't trade it for my independence. If you want to stay, fine. If not, I'll manage alone."

Drawn to her full height of five feet, eight inches, with her shoulders straight and her head back, she did her best to look absolutely determined. The casual work clothes she wore and the disarray of her long chestnut hair didn't help much. Nor did the tremulous weakness that urged her not to anger the people she cared so much about.

But she had no choice. Anger seemed to be all they understood. If she gave in now, to either Will or Lucas, she stood to lose everything. Stalwartly she faced them, resolved that no matter what it cost she would not let any man take charge of the decisions that were hers alone to make.

CHAPTER SIX

"Pass the salt, would you, Carly?" Timmy asked, a bit cautiously. Everyone was in an uncertain mood since returning from town. Those who had remained behind—Ma, Pa, and Gramma—weren't sure yet what had caused such prickly feelings, but they were treading warily around that particular thorn bush.

"Weather's been milder than usual for this time of year," Pa observed. "Ought to take advantage of it. Winter'll be here 'fore we know it."

"Pearson's having a sale on paint," Will mentioned. "Maybe we ought to buy some and do the barn now."

"Thought we were goin' to let that wait till spring," Timmy said.

Pa shrugged, helping himself to another serving of boiled potatoes. "No sense putting off to next year what we can get done now."

Silence reigned at the table for several minutes more until Gramma decided she'd had enough of it and snorted disparagingly. "You youngsters want to tell us what's going on?"

"Nothing," Carly insisted quickly.

"Everything's fine," Will claimed.

"Right as rain." This from Timmy who, perhaps because he was the youngest, managed to look the least convincing.

Rachel's usually soft mouth tightened as she looked at her brood. "If this is fine, I'd hate to see you three get upset. Ever since you got back from town, you've all been jumpier than chickens sitting in a skillet."

Will forked another pork chop onto his plate and smiled reassuringly. "That's just your imagination, Ma. We got a lot of work done today on Carly's place. It's shaping up real well."

Seth glanced at his wife in a silent exchange. His glance slid back to his children skeptically. "That's nice, but something sure seems to have got your dander up. Here Carly's been back only a few days and you're getting along no better than you did when you were kids."

Katie shot a quick warning look at her husband, but not in time to stop him from muttering, "How can you expect us to be getting along when she and Lucas Murdock are acting like long-lost friends?"

Carly set her milk glass down with a thud. "We are not!"

"Oh, no? Then what was all that stuff this afternoon about having the same goals and his asking you to work with him?"

"Plain common sense, which you'd be able to recognize if you weren't so bullheaded!"

"Lucas Murdock?" Pa repeated. "What in darnation does he have to do with this?"

"He was at Carly's place," Will explained. "Seems he took the store next door for his law practice. Came over to see how she was getting on."

"Right neighborly of him," Gramma muttered, her tone making it clear she thought anything but that.

Carly took a deep breath, willing herself to stay calm. She didn't want an argument, nor did she think she could let the conversation go any farther without getting a few things out in the open. "I know this upsets all of you," she began quietly. "Will and Timmy have already made their feelings quite clear. It's no secret that I don't share your opinion of the Murdocks, but I respect your right to think as you do. I'd appreciate it if you would give me the same courtesy."

Eyes shifted uneasily around the table as the Hanlons considered her request. It was left to Pa to respond for them all. Gently, in that patient voice of his, he said, "I don't rightly see what courtesy has to do with it, Carly. The Murdocks are trouble. We don't want you hurt by any of them. Is that so hard to understand?"

Her throat tightened painfully. It was impossible to doubt the sincerity of his concern. Yet she could not believe that it was justified. "I realize what you're saying, Pa. I just don't agree with you. Lucas is no threat to me, no more than his kin."

Gramma clucked her tongue impatiently as Rachel sighed. "Honey, we all know you're a real smart girl, getting through medical school and everything. But there's still parts of life you don't seem to know much about. The bad feelings between us and the Murdocks have festered over many a year. Do you really think they'd miss a chance to get back at us?"

Slowly, weighing her words, Carly said, "I think Lucas's father or his brothers might try to make things tough for us by knocking down some of our fences like they did a few winters back or trying to dam the creek to cut off our water. But I don't think they'd go any farther than that, certainly not as far as hurting one of us personally."

Timmy's disbelieving grimace was matched by his brother's. "You always did want to think the best of people," Will said, not sharply but as a simple statement of a fact they had all long ago accepted. "Maybe that's what makes you care enough to be such a good doctor."

Carly couldn't help but smile at that. They had no way of knowing what sort of doctor she was. Her smile faded as Will went on.

"But when it comes to the darker side of life, you need protecting. You did when you were little and I don't see any change in that now. Believe us, Carly, Lucas Murdock will hurt you if he can." Glancing at his mother and grandmother, he said, "Excuse me, but I'm going to speak bluntly. Lucas has wanted Carly since before she left here and that hasn't changed. I saw that today in the way he was looking at her. Going that long wanting something and not getting it can make the sweetest-tempered man mean."

Despite her best efforts to prevent it, Carly blushed. It was one thing to know inside her own heart that Will was right about Lucas's desires. It was quite another to have so personal a topic discussed in front of the family. For a moment she felt like a young girl again, uncertain of her own budding sensuality and unaware of how to cope with it.

Hard on the heels of that uncomfortable memory came the recollection of how far she had grown from the tremulous state of early womanhood. She was an adult now, able to make her own judgments and abide by them.

But able, too, to cherish her family as no child could ever do. The self-centered perceptions of earlier years were gone, replaced by a deep love and respect that both strengthened and weakened her. She could not give in to her family, nor could she hurt them.

"Look," she said quietly, "whatever Lucas does or does not feel for me really isn't the issue. The point is that we're both back here to help the community. We're not going to let ourselves be distracted by an old and worn-out feud. It's that simple."

Seth looked at his daughter for a long moment before he shook his head gently. "Nothing is ever that simple, Carly. Especially not when men and women are involved. If what Will says is true, and I suspect it is, you've got every reason to watch yourself around him."

Watch yourself. Carly liked the sound of that. It suggested that her father, at least, was willing to acknowledge that she was responsible for her own actions and their consequences. She nodded thoughtfully. "All right, I won't argue with that because it just isn't important to me. I'm here to work, and that's not going to leave much time for anything else."

"Doesn't take much time to get in trouble with a man like Lucas Murdock," Timmy muttered.

"That's enough," his father interjected quietly but with unmistakable firmness. "I think what Carly's trying to tell us is that she's not a little girl anymore. We trusted her to leave the Hollow and get the education she wanted. Now we can trust her on this too."

And that was that. Once Seth Hanlon had spoken, not even Gramma would challenge him. Carly beamed her father a grateful smile, but behind her apparent relief there was a rueful acknowledgment of having been outmaneuvered.

She had, in fact, assured them she wouldn't be having anything to do with Lucas. And that was one promise she knew she was going to be hard pressed to keep.

Just how difficult it was going to be to keep faith with her family became clear to her a short time later after the good nights were said and she went off to her room under the eaves. Sleep proved elusive, so much so that after tossing and turning for what seemed like hours, she gave up and sought some distraction.

Slipping into warm wool slacks and a pullover, she tucked her hair into a knit cap and tossed a sheepskin jacket over her shoulders. Outside the air was cool and clear, the night sky cloudless, with a waxing moon riding high above the trees.

It was very quiet in the clearing around the house. She could hear the rustling of the cows in the nearby barn and the flutter of an owl peering out from the roof of the woodshed. But another, more compelling sound called to her—the lapping of the lake against its rocky shore.

Skirting the main road, she headed along the path to the lower pasture, climbed over the stone wall that marked the boundary between Hanlon and Murdock land, and after a quick glance around continued on.

There couldn't be any danger. On such a night Lucas was undoubtedly snug in bed. Not necessarily his own, of course, but she wouldn't think of that. The lake had always been her special place. She had a hard time even remembering that strictly speaking it was enemy territory.

A shimmering ribbon of moonlight fell across the wide expanse of wine-dark water. Pine and fir trees came down almost to the shore, leaving only a narrow strip of alabaster sand studded by boulders like huge pieces of abstract sculpture deposited by a generous hand. Created by ancient forces, nestled under an eternal sky, no such beauty should—or could—be touched by the hatred of man.

Wind-tossed foam curled at her feet as she leaned

against one of the boulders, her eyes finding the place where long before Lucas had carved both their initials. He'd done it deliberately to provoke her, knowing she'd worry about her brothers discovering that evidence of their clandestine meetings. But had he also realized the far greater problem he caused her—whether or not to take him seriously?

A soft sigh escaped her as she let her fingers trace the carved reminders of youthful infatuation, on her part at least. She was grown-up now, far past the point of any adolescent crush or whatever it was she had felt for Lucas. And ready for . . . what . . . ?

If only they weren't who they were. A foolish hope wished for by how many people past and future? Their heritage was ingrained so deeply in them—like a vein of gold hidden far from the mortal eye—that it couldn't be ripped out at any cost. That was the final, absolute explanation for why they had both come back.

And having done so, what now? She shifted restlessly on the boulder. Too many questions, not enough answers. She should go back home, get into bed again, and not worry about things she couldn't settle.

Good advice, but about as practical to follow as the silver road of moonlight leading up into the sky.

She walked some little distance before pausing to pick up a small, flat rock. Her fingers curved around it automatically. Wondering if she remembered how, she sent it skimming across the water. It bounced half a dozen times before settling beneath the surface.

Her laughter was soft but carried far in the silence. Lucas had taught her to do that back when they were both children innocently determined to find the way to friendship, before all the complications of growing up beset them. He was a better teacher than she'd realized, judging by how she'd retained the skill.

Another stone skimmed the water, catching the moonlight like a jewel, teasing the surface that tried to hold it, rising two . . . three . . . four times into the midnight air before at last sinking.

Carly whirled, her heart in her throat, knowing what she would see and wishing she weren't quite so happy about it. Lucas stood just behind her, his eyes on the lake where the stone had vanished.

"I used to be better than that," he said quietly. "But you're still pretty good."

"That's the first time I got more than you," she reminded him, hardly aware of what she was saying. His presence blocked out all but the most automatic response.

Standing tall and dark against the sky, he looked as unshakable as any of the great trees that burrowed their roots into the ground and held on against all challenges. Yet there was also something tentative about him—in the way a lock of his hair fell across his forehead and his hands were jammed into his pockets—that made her want to reassure him.

That was just plain silly. He was the most self-confident man she had ever known. But why then did he look so uncertain, as though he weren't sure how she would react to him.

Cautiously resisting an urge to smile, Carly said, "Nice night for a walk."

"Is that what you're doing?"

"What else? I didn't come here to steal any Murdock fish."

He laughed, a rich sound that reverberated through her. "Remember the day I caught you doing that? You took off like someone had lit a fire under you, but I didn't let you get far."

Carly flushed, reliving in her mind that little episode from years past. She'd been fourteen, on the awkward edge between child and woman. Lucas had fascinated her. Though she hadn't admitted it then and wasn't about to now, she'd gone to the lake hoping to see him.

As an excuse, she'd boldly taken along her fishing rod and had the luck, if that was what it was, to catch two fair-size bass. Murdock bass, as Lucas hadn't hesitated to point out when he came upon her in the waning spring afternoon.

She'd run, all right, not because of any dumb fish, but because of the challenge that even then she'd been able to read in his eyes. And he'd come after her, catching her beneath the arching canopy of fir trees, tumbling her onto her back in the soft bed of needles, holding her down with his big, hard body until suddenly the nature of the struggle between them had changed and become what it had always been meant to be.

She could still recapture the flavor of his lips against hers and the texture of his kiss. He'd been very gentle, as though sensing she was on untried ground. But beneath the gentleness she'd felt the fire, the rampant male need to possess, and had been at once thrilled and frightened by it.

If it had been left up to her, the situation might well have gotten completely out of hand. But Lucas was older, wiser, and, for better or worse, compassionate. He'd let her go, despite his obvious arousal, and given her a warning she'd never forgotten.

"You're playing with fire, Carly Hanlon, and you don't even know it. If you have any sense, you'll keep your distance. Next time we're alone like this, I won't be responsible for what happens."

She'd trailed home forlornly, the fish forgotten, and for several months stayed away from the lake. But good intentions faded and old needs resurfaced. She and Lucas had met again, alone, and always between them was the memory of what had almost happened. But they'd managed, with only a few lapses, to keep from touching each other and igniting the tinder only waiting for the slightest spark to turn it into a raging inferno.

Until now. Across the short expanse of rock-strewn sand they faced each other. "If you're not here to fish," Lucas said softly, "why are you here?"

"To think. To try to resolve some old problems."

"I guess I don't have to ask what they are?"

"Probably not," she admitted, smiling despite herself. So many years they'd talked like this, on the edge of the dark water with only the moon and stars as witness. Somewhere along the way they'd lapsed into the comfortable shorthand of people who know each other far too well to need many words.

"I'm sorry about what happened today," he murmured, not taking his eyes from her. The moon was almost directly overhead, casting a luminescent glow on her delicate features.

"It doesn't matter. We talked it out over dinner."

"That must have been some meal."

She turned slightly, looking at the water, her shoulders hunched as though against the wind. He made her feel so full of yearning. "I suggested to them, very strongly, that I was only interested in my medical practice and that I wouldn't be seeing you"—she hesitated briefly—"except in the line of duty."

"Duty, hmmm? That covers all sorts of things."

"I didn't mean it that way."

"I know you didn't. But don't you agree we have a duty to ourselves?"

"To do what? Indulge our libidos?"

The question came out more harshly than she'd meant. He'd struck at the heart of her problem. She was no more anxious to betray herself than to betray her family. Left alone, she might have been able to pretend she didn't really want him. But confronted by the reality of her desire, she was helpless to deny it.

Did she imagine that he flinched? If so the motion was so slight that she all but missed it. He regained control of himself at once, his eyes cold and dark as they surveyed her remorselessly. "Is this what they taught you in the big city, how to hide from your feelings?"

"You should talk. I'm not the only one who was out there and learned what was being taught."

"That's no excuse. You can choose what you become. You don't have to give up on honesty."

"Are you saying you haven't?"

He took a step closer to her, goaded by the unbridled skepticism in her voice as much as by the vulnerable stance of her slender body. She had no idea how she looked to him—all silk and softness hiding fire. He wanted her so badly it hurt.

"If you've listened to anything at all that I've said since the night you came home, you know what I've been trying to tell you. Nothing's changed between us. Nothing at all. Now it's time to admit it, instead of running from the truth."

"Maybe you should do some listening yourself, Lucas. I've been telling you that nothing's changed as far as our families are concerned. Why won't you admit that?"

The anguish rippling through her words reached clear

through him. It brought everything down to the most fundamental level. He couldn't bear to see her hurt, not by him or anyone. Yet how to protect her when his very soul cried out to take what he wanted now and worry about the consequences later?

In the final analysis he was only a man, as strong—and as weak—in his own way as she was in hers. He claimed no greater insight into right and wrong, nor could he predict the outcome of whatever happened between them.

He knew only that life was, at best, a tenuous thing no more secure than a feather floating on a fast-rushing river. In an instant it could all be gone. How, then, to resist a chance at something strong and stable enough to stand against the current and give purpose to the flow of time?

Afterward he would ask himself why he hadn't had the courage to walk away. But just then nothing mattered except to defy the forces arrayed against them and brand her with the same immutable fire that had burned within him through all the long years they'd spent apart.

CHAPTER SEVEN

Carly told herself she had nothing to worry about. No matter how much Lucas might want to give in to the fierce desire she saw smoldering in his eyes, he couldn't change the fact that they were standing out in the open on a none-too-warm night with no protection and no guarantee of privacy. Hardly the place to make love. Even he would have to recognize that and admit defeat.

Too late she remembered the cabin. Long abandoned by fishermen who once worked the lake, it had been a playhouse for her and Lucas when they were children. But that was years ago. It couldn't possibly still be standing, could it?

She turned around, carefully studied the screen of trees that had grown higher since she had last been there, and caught sight of it. The cabin was still there, sheltered from the wind and prying eyes, seeming to wait for them.

Carly took a step backward, heedless of the water that promptly seeped into her shoes. "I think I'd better be getting home."

He smiled gently, letting her know he knew everything

that was going through her mind. "No." One word, so simple and so absolute. He didn't even raise his voice. Instead, he simply walked toward her, his intent clear in every step he took.

Pride demanded that she hide her fear, and her excitement. She had been heading toward this moment all her life, half believing it would never happen, half hoping to hurry its arrival. Now that it was at last upon her she had no idea what to do.

Lucas had no such problem. The hands that reached for her were infinitely gentle, yet unmistakably firm. Through the soft wool of her jacket and shirt, she could feel the warmth of his fingers. As he drew her toward him, she glanced up, studying his features with a wary intensity that plucked a cord deep within him.

"There's nothing to be afraid of," he murmured huskily. "You know that."

Did she? He looked so . . . sure of himself . . . and of her. She resented that, even as the woman in her responded to it.

His arm slipped around her shoulder, drawing her to him. "It's getting colder. Come on."

She didn't have to ask where he was leading her. The path to the cabin was overgrown with weeds, but still usable. The door creaked stiffly as Lucas pushed it open. Something fluttered amid the beams of the ceiling in protest at their sudden intrusion.

Glancing up, Carly found herself eye to eye with a perturbed barn owl. The little creature, no bigger than a soda can, blinked at her censoriously, ruffled its feathers, and darted off toward a dark corner of the cabin.

Lucas's soft laugh rumbled against her cheek. "Not bad, as audiences go. At least we know he won't talk."

That *was* an important point. She knew perfectly well

that by going with him to the cabin, she was committing herself to a course of action they both desired. Not for a moment did she reconsider that commitment, but she still wasn't ready for it to become public knowledge.

She moved slightly, out of his arms, to put some distance between them in the hope it would help her think more clearly. "There's a lot we'll have to discuss, Lucas. You know that."

He nodded somberly, his gaze never leaving her. She was struck by the hunger in his eyes, and by the tenderness. "We will," he promised quietly. "We'll work everything out."

Carly believed him. But then she really didn't have any choice. Not when every part of her was crying out for the fulfillment so long denied and at last within reach.

Standing so close to him in the shadowed cabin, listening to the murmur of the wind outside and the rustle of the pine trees, she knew her homecoming had not ended when she stepped from the jeep into the arms of her parents. There was another home to return to, barely acknowledged yet always there in the back of her mind and the deep currents of her spirit. Lucas.

She remembered him as a child, laughing at the sky. She recalled him as a young man, alien and frightening to her, sparking resentment at the transformation inevitable in them both. Now the rough edges of youth were gone, replaced by the steady certainty of who he was and what he wanted. A certainty she shared.

A stone fireplace took up one corner of the cabin. Lucas knelt in front of it, neatly stacking the logs and tinder he found nearby. When he was satisfied that it would burn well, he took a matchbook from his pocket. Cupping the flame in the hollow of his hand, he leaned forward to set it carefully against the wadded up newspapers. They caught instantly. Within minutes a bright fire was taking the chill of the cabin and filling it with warmth.

He turned, beckoning to her. "Come and sit down."

There was a braided rug in front of the fireplace. It was surprisingly clean, as was the entire cabin. Joining him, she frowned slightly. "Someone's been using this place."

Lucas drew her closer, nestling her head against his chest. She offered no resistance. His strength comforted her, easing the tension from her limbs and her soul.

He pressed a light kiss against the crown of her hair before he murmured, "I have a confession to make. I stopped by here earlier and cleaned the place up."

Carly stared into the flames, hoping he couldn't see her smile. No sense letting him be too confident right off the bat. "Why? Were you so sure I'd come here?"

"No, but you can't blame a man for hoping."

"Hmmm." She had a feeling Lucas did more than just hope. He was too resolute to sit back and let events unfold without his influence. Maybe chance had led her to the lake that night. But honesty forced her to admit that sooner or later she would have ended up at exactly the same point.

Settling more comfortably into his arms, she asked, "While you were tidying up, did you happen to find any amenities suitable for a chilly autumn night?"

Some of the tension eased from him as he heard the humorous acceptance in her voice and knew she wasn't angered by his foresight. "As a matter of fact, I believe there's a bottle of rather good brandy in that cupboard over there."

While he spoke, he lowered her to the rug, cradling her gently as his lips brushed lightly against the curve of her cheek. The caress was light as a feather, the touch of a dream lover. Yet the tremor of pleasure that raced through her was unmistakably real.

Beneath her jacket and shirt her breasts swelled; the nipples became taut and aching. A hot, sweet bolt of yearning licked at her, provoking a soft moan.

Lucas smiled down at her, his burnished features taut with need and his cerulean eyes alight with the pleasure of a man who hears the primeval response of his chosen woman and knows its meaning.

He stared at the mouth from which the soft sound had come, as though fascinated by the ripe moistness of her lips. Carefully, holding his great strength and urgent need in strict check, he leaned forward, letting his breath mingle with hers.

It wasn't a kiss, exactly. It was more like a long, lingering tasting and savoring. Carly had never experienced anything like it. She was being devoured, tenderly and with her full cooperation.

Fragmented thoughts darted through her mind. Lucas was a highly experienced man, more than capable of fulfilling her greatest needs. But he was also vulnerable. She could feel that in him. He wanted not only to have his passion accepted, but also returned. In full.

She did not disappoint him. They melded together as naturally as though their separation into two distinct individuals had been merely an oversight of nature. The beating of their hearts, the coursing of blood through their veins, the internal rhythms of life itself were all in perfect synchrony.

The brandy was forgotten, as were all other trappings of seduction. None were needed when both were in such absolute accord.

Carly did not want to be wooed. She wanted to be possessed by him. She wanted to yield herself entirely when she took him into her and made him a part of her in the most fundamental way possible.

Lucas undressed her with poignant intensity. Her shirt quickly followed her jacket, falling forgotten into the shadows beyond the rug. Not expecting to meet anyone, she hadn't bothered with a bra. Honeyed skin set off by nipples as pink as the petals of a fully ripe rose, her breasts flowed into his hands.

She felt, as well as heard, his sharply indrawn breath. "Lord, but you're beautiful, Carly. Just as I knew you would be."

It was no practiced lover's compliment, but it rang of truth, as he perceived it. In his eyes, beneath his hands, she was beautiful. Did any other judgment matter?

As impatient to discover him as he was her, she fumbled with the buttons of his shirt. Her fingers were stiff, their movement unpracticed. Lucas laughed deep in his throat. Her lack of expertise told him something precious about the years she had spent away from the Hollow, something that touched him to the very core of his being.

His feelings for Carly had always surprised him, not only in their strength but in their uniqueness. With her he experienced a part of himself no one else had ever uncovered. With no other woman had he known such unbridled passion coupled with aching tenderness. With no one else was he driven to possess solely and completely.

When his shirt at last fell open, she sighed with mingled relief and pleasure. His chest was broad and tautly muscled, covered by a thick ebony pelt that tapered into a dark line disappearing beneath the low-slung waistband of his jeans. Leaning forward, she let her nipples rub lightly against the downy curls.

The effect on Lucas was immediate and highly satisfying. He made a guttural sound deep in his throat as he grasped her shoulders, pressing her back onto the rug. His callused hands quickly disposed of her remaining clothes, until she was left with nothing more than a tiny scrap of silk and lace shielding her womanhood from his hungry eyes.

"I didn't want to rush this," he groaned as he moved away from her just long enough to yank off the rest of his clothes. "But I can't help myself. You're so lovely . . . so much a part of me . . ."

The husky uncertainty she heard in his voice pierced Carly all the way through. Without having to be told, she understood the conflict tearing at him. He wanted their lovemaking to be perfect for her, but he wasn't certain he could hold himself back long enough to assure that.

A soft, infinitely female smile curved her mouth. If only he knew how unnecessary his concern was. Never had she been as prepared for anything as she was for the ultimate culmination that was at last within her reach.

Opening her arms to him, she told him wordlessly all that lay within her heart and mind. Lucas hesitated only an instant longer, as though not daring to believe the truth of what he beheld. Then the passion flowing like quicksilver between them overcame him and he gathered her close, cradling her with fierce strength against the rugged masculinity of his body.

Never had Carly felt so tenderly cherished or so ruthlessly claimed. The sheer power of burnished skin and steely muscle overwhelmed her. She was engulfed in raw virility, swept away on a rushing current of liquid fire. His lean, hard fingers slipped beneath the band of her last garment, urging it from her, then pausing to gently explore all that he had revealed.

Never had she been so breathtakingly aware of herself

as a woman and of the explosive force hidden within her, only waiting to be unlocked by the man who loomed over her. His slightest touch shattered the bounds of her self-restraint and turned her into a writhing creature mindlessly seeking the release only he could give.

As his tongue plunged ravenously within her mouth, her fingers dug into his shoulders and her hips lifted against him in unconscious pleading. The sweet feint and parry presaging the ultimate act of love drove her hunger to new and unbearable heights.

She cried out softly as his lips explored the slender line of her throat and gently rounded shoulders even as his rough-silk thigh pressed between hers, opening her for him.

Big hands cupped her breasts, squeezing lightly, his thumbs rubbing again and again over her rigid nipples. Her long chestnut hair flowed in a satiny tangle over the rug as she shook her head from side to side helplessly.

"Lucas . . . please . . ."

He laughed deep in his throat, prompting a spurt of bittersweet ire that faded instantly beneath the remorseless demand of his caresses. Despite the raging torrent of his own need, Lucas withheld what she so desperately craved. He took her to the brink of fulfillment again and again, only to draw back at the final moment, leaving her stretched taut by a force she could barely comprehend and not at all control.

The fire raged higher, sending showers of sparks up the chimney. The wind whistled round the tops of tall pine trees and tried unsuccessfully to edge in between the cabin's snugly fitted logs. The moon set, leaving the night sky to the vast panoply of stars. Jupiter, almost a sun in its own right, lay to the south. Shimmering Pegasus rode eastward. To the west Arcturus hung poised. Lovely Cassiopeia hung overhead, bright even against the vivid swatch of the Milky Way racing away into infinity.

The stars, so brilliant in the mind's eye, were as nothing to the galaxy of fire and heat exploding within her. Carly cried out again, pierced by a multitude of sensations. She was losing herself, dissolving in a fulminating that radiated outward until she was engulfed and cast high into a realm she had never before glimpsed.

And she was not alone. Lucas was with her as surely as their bodies were at last joined, as completely as they took and gave the ultimate in pleasure and fulfillment. Then it was she who was strong as he trembled in her arms, crying out her name, as his power left him in a vast, pulsating rush, coming to her as a gift of life and love everlasting.

A gift she fully returned in the timeless moments when the inner universe of their hearts and souls shattered around them and like the fragments of a kaleidoscope reformed into a new, more beautiful whole.

CHAPTER EIGHT

"I said we'd talk," Lucas murmured reluctantly, "but to be honest, that's the farthest thing from my mind right now."

"I know." Carly sighed, stirring in his arms. She sat up slightly, just enough to look at him. In the darting firelight his skin shone like molten bronze. His features were more relaxed than she had ever seen them. The firm line of his mouth was softened and his eyes were tender. The warm plaid blanket he had pulled over them covered him only to his flat stomach. The rest of him was bare to her appreciative gaze.

She smiled wryly as a wave of fresh longing washed over her. Moments after reaching the heights of fulfillment, her body was already coming alive again. "I don't want to worry you," she said lightly, "but I think I may be insatiable."

A straight black eyebrow rose teasingly. "Really?"

He sounded so hopeful that she couldn't resist taking a playful swat at him. Catching her wrist, he drew her hand against his chest, nuzzling her fingers into the thick pelt of hair she had delighted in discovering.

Deep in his throat he growled, "Behave yourself, woman." As though to emphasize his command, a long, muscular leg moved over her satiny limbs, holding her in gentle entrapment. His other hand became entangled in her silken hair, cupping the back of her head. Their hips moved against each other longingly, provoking a stifled moan from Carly.

"Behave *myself?* Isn't that the pot calling the kettle black?"

Not even the dim light of the cabin could hide his slashing grin. "Are you suggesting," he drawled, "that a friendly embrace has some . . . untoward effect on you?"

She nodded energetically. "Told you I was insatiable."

"Thank heaven!"

"Besides, if that's your idea of friendly, you must have had quite a speckled career these last few years."

"On the contrary," he murmured, suddenly serious. "I can't deny that I played the field a bit, but never with any great degree of enthusiasm. Memories of a certain green-eyed hill beauty kept getting in the way."

She laughed unrepentantly. "How frustrating for you."

"Exactly." Bending her back over his sinewy arm, he glared down at her with mock ferocity. "I expect you to make up for every single moment of it."

The blanket slipped away, revealing her breasts still full and taut from his loving. Lucas's gaze shifted as a pulse leaped to life in the shadowed hollow of his cheek.

"Let's see now," Carly murmured as he bent his head to nuzzle her smooth throat. "That should take about ten years."

She held her breath, thinking he would say something

noncommittal, only to let it go as he muttered, "More. I'm charging interest."

"At exorbitant rates, I hope?"

"Usurious."

"What big words we know."

"That's how lawyers get to charge so much."

"Is that what you do, charge a lot?"

"Used to, in the big city." His tongue darted out to stroke the sprinkling of freckles on her shoulder. "Made a bundle. Don't need any more."

That was good, if he was really serious about setting up practice in the Hollow. "Lucas . . . that store you rented . . . is it . . . permanent?"

He looked up, their eyes meeting. His were stormy with renewed passion that faded slightly as he took in her concern and aptly judged its cause. Gently, he framed her face in his big hands as he said, "I'm not leaving, Carly. This is where I belong, just as you do. We're where we were always supposed to be, in this place, in each other's lives."

She swallowed hard, fighting the sudden rush of sad-happy tears. "There are people who would disagree with you."

"And they're all named Hanlon or Murdock."

"That's about it."

"Well . . . we could both change our names."

She laughed damply. "So logical. Why didn't I think of that?"

"How does 'Handock' strike you, or maybe 'Murlon'?"

"Ghastly."

Turning over onto his back, he drew her with him and stared up at the ceiling thoughtfully. "All kidding aside, we do have a problem. Our families can't be kept in the dark forever."

"No . . . but I don't think it would be a good idea to spring this on them without any preparation."

"Sometimes a shock can really help. It cures the hiccups, doesn't it?"

Propping herself up on an elbow, she studied him quietly. Despite his attempts at lightness, he obviously understood the seriousness of their predicament. Neither of them could bear to hurt the families they loved, nor could they walk away from the joy they had discovered together. A compromise was needed . . . at least temporarily.

Slowly, she said, "Maybe we could break it to them gradually . . . take it a step at a time so that they have a chance to get used to what's happening."

He turned slightly, touching a gentle hand to the soft curve of her cheek. Such a small gesture, yet so filled with tenderness. She took a deep breath, willing her head to stay clear, if only long enough to devise a plan.

"I know I told my brothers that I wouldn't be working with you, but since our practices are going to be right next door to each other, isn't it sort of inevitable that we'd cooperate?"

"That's what I've been trying to tell you all along," he pointed out quietly.

"I know . . . I just didn't think it was possible."

"And now?"

She looked at him for a long moment, drinking in the firm strength and purpose of his features and the calm steadiness of his gaze, before she said, "Now I don't seem to have any choice."

The sudden flare of satisfaction and relief that darted through his eyes made her smile ruefully. "But you knew that all along, didn't you?"

"Let's just say I hoped."

"Hmmm. While you're looking so pleased with yourself, how about some of that brandy you mentioned?"

He looked down at her in teasing disbelief. "But that's all the way over there on the other side of the room. I'll freeze."

"Not," she informed him succinctly, "if you hurry."

With an exaggerated sigh and a muttered comment about the whims of women, Lucas eased himself from beneath the covers and strode swiftly across the cabin. Carly watched him with unconcealed pleasure. He was so beautifully made that she could not take her eyes from him.

Firelight caressed the sculpted planes and hollows of his powerful body, emphasizing the fluid lines of muscle and sinew. He moved with innate grace and power. The proud carriage of his superbly male form proclaimed him to be in his prime. The desk work of a lawyer had in no way softened him. He was all lean hardness and virile strength.

There was an elemental maleness about him, shorn as he was of the usual trappings of civilization that tended to obscure the fundamental differences between the sexes. Without his clothes, in the quiet seclusion of the cabin, he might have been a man of an earlier age, recently satisfied by his woman and content for the moment to show the more tractable side of his nature.

Even the crystal goblets he withdrew from the cabinet had the aura of another era. Snuggling down under the blanket, Carly smiled at her imaginings. She had never considered herself prone to flights of fancy, but with Lucas she was discovering previously unsuspected aspects of her personality.

Swept away by the resonating echoes of languorous fulfillment, she was willing, at least for the moment, to let him set the pace between them. Later the more assertive side of her nature would undoubtedly show itself, with predictably pleasant results. But just then it was enough to lie back against their impromptu bed and let him do as he would.

"I think you'll like this," he said, pouring a generous measure of brandy into each of the goblets.

A glance at the bottle was enough to tell Carly he was right. Trust Lucas to choose a very old, very rare vintage with which to celebrate their union. Letting a few drops of the silken fire trickle down her throat, she smiled appreciatively.

"I could get very used to this."

Twirling an imaginary mustache, he chuckled villainously. "My plan seems to be working. Soon, my beauty, you will be too dazzled with sensual delights to deny me anything."

Carly laughed wryly. "I'm in no shape to do that now."

Leering suggestively, he moved closer under the covers. "Good. Then you'll give me what I want."

Despite herself, Carly giggled, a highly unusual sound for her. He looked so roguish with a lock of ebony hair falling over his brow and his eyes alight with ribald mischief. In pretended fright, she tried to draw back, only to be stopped by the sudden touch of something icy cold against her legs.

"Lucas! What's that?"

"My feet, of course," he informed her blandly. "You beat a hot water bottle any day."

"Thanks heaps!"

Trying unsuccessfully to wriggle away from him, Carly managed to splash a few drops of brandy on his chest. She stared at them thoughtfully. "Messy."

"Extremely. What are you going to do about it?"

"Well, since I don't happen to have paper towels or a washcloth . . ." She leaned forward, her hair brushing like warm silk over his arms and chest. The male scent of him filled her nostrils. She inhaled deeply, savoring the rush of near dizzying need.

Lucas held himself very still. He made no effort to guide her, only waited for her instincts to do their part. A groan escaped him as he discovered she required no instruction.

Her tongue was soft and wet against his skin as she lapped away the drops of brandy, moving over him like a small kitten relishing a treat. Long after the last trace of the spill was gone, she continued her explorations. The scent and texture of him delighted her; the taste of him was an elixir she could not resist; and the discoveries she was making prompted her to go farther and farther.

For all the differences in their relative levels of experience, he was by no means immune to her efforts. A soft, definitely female laugh of sheer pleasure rose within her as she realized just how very susceptible he could be.

There was enchantment in the knowledge of the power she could wield over this powerful, dominant male. He trembled beneath her, his big hands clenched into fists at his side as he fought the need to take hold of her, letting her build his anticipation—and hers—to nearly unendurable heights.

But even his vast self-control had limits, as she discovered. At some point—impossible to say where—her caresses changed from enthralled fascination to a very feminine, very deliberate provocation. Dimly in the back of her mind Carly was aware of what she was doing and was startled by it. She could never have imagined herself in the role of temptress, yet that seemed to be exactly what she had become.

Part of her was quite amused by her daring, but another viewed the matter with complete seriousness. Beneath all the gentle tenderness of their loving, an inherent challenge existed. They were testing each other as only a man and woman could do. Ruthless as it sounded, she wanted to take Lucas to his absolute limits and beyond.

That she had achieved her goal became startlingly evident when a harsh groan escaped him and he moved with decisive speed to right the imbalance between them. Work-roughened hands grasped her waist. The room turned head over heels until she felt the warmth of the rug beneath her back. Her breath caught as she looked up at him, seeing the proof of her effectiveness in the sharpness of his features and the fire burning in his eyes.

"Time for lesson two," he grated. "What happens when you push a man too far."

For all his fierceness, she could not find it in herself to be afraid. Instead she lay under him trustingly, offering no resistance as his hard thigh pushed apart her own thighs, and his seeking hand quickly found the center of her desire.

He hesitated a moment, long enough to make sure she could accept him without discomfort. That consideration even in the face of his overwhelming need touched her deeply. Without restraint, her hips arched closer to him and she silently urged him to enter her.

When he did so, she cried out with pleasure. This was what she wanted more than anything, to be joined with him in the most intimate way possible and to share, if only briefly, the exquisite sense of being one flesh and one spirit.

Yet even at the height of their union, when the world

dissolved around them and time itself seemed to cease to exist, a tiny voice deep within her questioned how long such perfection could last, especially when confronted with all the sad memories of the past and the enduring hostilities of the present.

CHAPTER NINE

"If you'll give her the pills three times a day," Carly said reassuringly, "and make sure she stays warm, she should be fine by the end of the week."

Emily nodded gratefully, cradling the little girl who had stopped fussing and slipped into sleep. "Thank heaven. I've been so worried about her."

"Of course you have. But believe me she looked far worse than she really is. It's just a cold complicated by the normal difficulties of teething. With the medicine, she'll be able to sleep, which means you will too."

Studying her friend, Carly couldn't help but think that the other woman needed rest every bit as much as her ailing child. Emily's pale face was pinched and there were dark shadows under her eyes. It was natural that she should be worried about little Adeline, but something else also seemed to be bothering her.

With the door to the examining room closed, she felt able to ask quietly, "Is there anything else wrong . . . a problem we could talk about?"

Emily glanced up at her, startled. A slight flush stained

her cheeks. She hesitated, seemingly torn between natural reticence and the need to unburden herself. Carly's sympathetic manner combined with her intrinsic authority as a doctor won out.

"It's the mine," the young woman said softly. "Jim and some of the other men are real worried about conditions down there. They've been trying for months to get the owners to pay attention, but they haven't had any luck. Now some of them are talking about going to Lucas for help."

Carly nodded thoughtfully. Jim was Emily's husband, a strong, quiet man not given to exaggeration. If he believed there was danger below ground, then that was undoubtedly the case.

Her mouth tightened as she considered how often it had happened before; men's lives were placed in danger and frequently lost because safety measures were sacrificed to profits.

"I'm sure Lucas could do something for them," she said. "Have they made up their minds to consult him?"

"No . . . not exactly. You see the mine manager got wind of what was going on and let it be known that Lucas was off limits. He's threatened to suspend any man seen going into Lucas's office."

"He can't do that! People do have rights, and meeting with whomever one wants to is one of them."

Emily smiled sadly. "Maybe that's true out in the world, but you know it isn't the way of the Hollow. Here the bosses have always had the last word about everything."

Carly couldn't deny that, but she could take a certain fierce pride in the fact that the status quo was changing. Her friend's willingness to mention the problem to her was proof of that.

"If I could arrange for some way for your husband and the other men to meet with Lucas without the mine manager finding out, would they go along?"

Emily thought about that for a moment before slowly nodding. "Yes, I think they're desperate enough to take a chance. But how could you . . . ?"

"Leave that to me. I'll let you know this afternoon."

Still curious but too polite to press the matter, Emily left a short time later. Several other patients passed through the examining room, a gratifyingly large number considering the fact that Carly had opened her practice only two weeks ago.

At first, the days had dragged as only one or two people came by. But slowly resistance to her was wearing down.

She had no illusions that this was because people in the Hollow had any great faith in her. It was simply because they were desperate. Medical problems had long gone untreated, and Carly knew that pain and fear were responsible for filling her waiting room.

Eventually, after she dealt with the most chronic problems, she hoped people would come to her for routine checkups and preventive medicine. But that was a long way off.

First she had to cope with the generations of neglect and hopelessness. That was a problem she couldn't solve alone, especially if many of the people she had come to help were working under hazardous conditions in the mines.

When her last patient had gone, Carly closed the door to the infirmary and drew down the blinds. Taking off her white coat, she put it in her bag for laundering, then spent a few minutes straightening the waiting room, putting her instruments away in the sterilizer, and generally tidying up.

A slight smile touched her eyes as she considered that doctors rarely did such mundane chores. They expected others to clean up after them, but that was a luxury she gladly did without. Those of her patients who could afford to do so paid a few dollars; many she saw without charge.

Yet so far as money went, she was doing better than she had expected—partly because her parents insisted on providing free room and board, but also because Lucas had overridden her objections and bought the furnishings for the waiting room as well as various other incidentals that made the infirmary more comfortable for both her and her patients.

She had been reluctant to take his help at first, until he accused her of putting pride before the welfare of those she had come to help. That stung, all the more because it had been true.

Relenting, she had accepted what he gave and found in that acceptance an unexpected measure of comfort. She was not alone in the challenges she faced. No matter how tough it got, Lucas understood and shared her feelings.

They quickly fell into the routine of meeting every evening to discuss the day's events, those encounters leading more often than not to lovemaking on the wide comfortable couch he had sensibly installed in his office. In that way they nourished each other and stored up their strength for the struggles ahead.

Thinking of him, she felt the now-familiar rush of warmth through her body. He was so much a man—strong yet tender, demanding yet giving. Unself-conscious in his need for her, he shared not only the power of his body but also the restless, surging drive of his mind and spirit.

As she slipped into her fleece jacket and smoothed her hair, she considered what the last few weeks had been like for him. While her practice grew quickly, Lucas's was stagnating. No one, not even a potential client, had walked through his office doors.

They had talked about that just the night before. Lucas wasn't surprised; he had correctly anticipated the reluctance that would keep even those with the most legitimate complaints from seeking him out.

He had taken pains to be available elsewhere besides the confines of his official place of business. Yet the casual encounters around town that should have helped ease doubts about him did not seem to be having the intended effect.

After listening to Emily, Carly understood why. Lucas was facing more than simply the normal reticence he had expected. The mine manager was actively working against him, threatening those who would normally have sought his help.

Slipping out the back door of the infirmary, she walked the short distance to the adjacent building and entered through the rear door. Lucas's office was at the head of the stairs. She knocked and went in, finding him standing with his back to her, staring out the window.

For a moment Carly was content simply to look at him. Dressed as usual in jeans and a workshirt no different from those worn by almost every other man in town, including her father and brothers, he still managed to look like no one she had ever before encountered.

A wry smile curved her mouth as she considered that the mere sight of him was enough quite literally to knock the breath from her. All the clichés of love were proving true in her case. Except when she was with her patients, she tended to walk around in a daze, viewing the world through rose-tinted lenses.

The sound of his voice was enough to send tremors racing through her. The slightest touch of his hand made her arch instinctively closer. And when they did truly come together, the wonder of what they shared pierced her to the very core of her being.

Only their continued concern about the enmity between their families kept them from ever being completely happy and completely forthright about their love. The strain of keeping secret such a tumult of emotions was increasingly difficult. Added to their worries about the Hollow in general, the tension was slowly becoming almost unendurable.

With his hands in his pockets and his feet planted slightly apart, Lucas should have looked relaxed as he surveyed the scene out the window. But instead his big body silently communicated a sense of unease and mounting concern.

Forcing herself to smile, Carly said gently, "I've come to take you away from all this."

He turned, giving her just a glimpse of the bleakness in his eyes before it gave way to pleasure at seeing her. She blushed slightly as his gaze wandered over her appreciatively, prompting him to laugh softly. "That's the best offer a man could have."

His hands came out of his pockets; his arms opened naturally to her. She went into them with the same sense of homecoming she experienced every time they saw each other after even the briefest separation. His embrace was hungry, telling her something more about the unhappy thoughts he was trying so stalwartly to hide.

Nestled against him, breathing in the scent of his crisp,

clean shirt combined with the subtle, natural aroma of his skin, she felt a fierce sense of pride in his need for her, and a determination to do everything she possibly could to help him.

Backing away slightly, she met the quizzical look in his eyes with a reassuring smile as she said, "Let's sit down. We have to talk."

As they sat side by side on the couch where they had so often made love, she had to muster all her willpower to concentrate on what she meant to say. His nearness there in the quiet room made her forgetful. Taking a deep breath, she resolved to muddle through.

"Emily Hawkins came to see me today. Her little girl, Adeline, was ailing. After I took care of her, Emily mentioned that her husband, Jim, and several other men are very worried about conditions in the mine. They've wanted to come and talk with you about it, but the manager of the mine has made it clear that if they do, they're liable to lose their jobs."

His eyebrows rose slightly. "Somebody should tell him this is the twentieth century."

"Exactly what I suggested to Emily. But she reminded me how much power the bosses have. The men have reason to be concerned. They can't afford to lose their jobs."

Lucas sighed softly. "The same threat has been used for years. I won't deny that there were times when it carried some force, but nowadays it's not that easy to find men to work the mines. The owners aren't so foolish as to believe they can indulge in wholesale firings without destroying their business."

"No, but perhaps they think they could fire just a few men, make an example of them, and the rest would knuckle under."

"Not," Lucas said firmly, "if they were properly organized." He looked at her speculatively. "Which, I presume, is what this is all about?"

She grinned unrepentantly. "Of course. Since the men can't come to you at this point, I thought perhaps you could meet with them at the infirmary. They can't get into trouble for coming to see a doctor and since our . . . relationship . . . isn't common knowledge yet, I don't think the manager would get suspicious."

"You're probably right," he admitted. "But I don't like the idea of your taking such a risk."

Carly smothered a sigh. The protectiveness she saw in him so often was usually no more than a pleasing reminder of his feelings for her, but occasionally he stepped over the boundary between wanting to care for her and intruding on her ability to make her own decisions and look after herself.

She sought for some way to explain that without hurting him. "Lucas . . . I can make up my mind for myself about what I will and won't do. This problem with the mine concerns me as much as anyone else in the Hollow. There's no way I'll sit back and pretend it doesn't exist."

For a moment she thought he would get his back up at her show of defiance, but after frowning briefly, Lucas shook his head wryly and grinned. "I might have known I wouldn't get away with that. Sorry."

Carly laughed and touched his hand lightly. They understood each other so perfectly. She couldn't believe everything wouldn't work out well for them. "That's all right, just so long as we're straight on it now. I'll call Emily and arrange for Jim and the others to come to the infirmary this evening. Okay?"

"Fine. Do you have any idea how many will attend?"

"No, I don't. But from what Emily told me, I'd guess

there's a great deal of concern. The turnout should be good."

In fact, it was better than that. By eight o'clock some three dozen men had crammed their way into the infirmary's small waiting room. They stood about talking among themselves, their deep voices tight with concern and the normal fatigue that accompanied the end of yet another long, grueling day underground.

The shades of windows fronting on Main Street were pulled down, but the light could be clearly seen through them. A sign on the door announced that Carly was having evening office hours. Anyone passing by without knowing what was happening would have concluded an epidemic had suddenly hit Spruce Hollow.

As she moved among the men, exchanging a few words with those she knew and introducing herself to the strangers, Carly was struck by the fact that she was the only woman present. The wives who had spread the word about the meeting were at home. This was men's business.

They were leery of Lucas; to those who remembered him he was the wild Murdock young'un who left the Hollow. To others he was still very much a stranger. Yet in their desperation, they were at least willing to give him a chance to help them.

As the meeting began, Carly took a place in the back of the room where she could listen and observe without being obtrusive. Jim Hawkins, Emily's husband, called the men to order.

"You all know why we're here. Conditions in the mine have reached the point where every day we go without a serious accident is a miracle. If we want to prevent real injuries—or worse—we've got to act now."

The men nodded their agreement as one of them said,

"It's the new management that's caused this. Pete Wilcox is so hot to show a big profit that he's cutting back on safety."

"Not that the owners have ever cared much about safe working conditions," another pointed out. "But at least they obeyed the laws. Wilcox isn't even doing that."

"True enough," Jim agreed. "And that's why we're looking to the law to help us." He gestured to Lucas, turning the meeting over to him.

Carly could not suppress a flash of pride as she watched him move to the front of the room. He looked so sure of himself and so determined. Something of his confidence and sincerity must have reached the other men, for there was a brief murmur of approval before he began to speak.

"Jim and some of the rest of you have explained to me what's going on in the mines. There's no doubt federal safety regulations are being violated, and it seems clear that the problem started shortly after Wilcox took over. My understanding of the situation is that he's insecure about holding on to his new position, so he's doing everything he can to impress his bosses, at your expense."

"So what can we do about him?" one of the men demanded. "We've tried complaining to headquarters, but we just get ignored."

"The owners of the mine will stand behind management," Lucas said quietly, "until it becomes absolutely impossible for them to continue to do so. My advice is to begin by approaching Wilcox. Let me talk to him. I'll make it clear as your representative that his threats aren't going to work. He'll get a chance to clean up conditions—quickly. If he fails, we go to the owners and demand his replacement."

Several men nodded, but others were vocal in their

objections. "If you let Wilcox know we've talked to you, he'll fire us. He's got the authority to do that."

"There is a danger he might try to get rid of some of you," Lucas admitted. "But not if you stand firmly together. There are enough men here tonight to form the nucleus of a strike. We should agree right now that if one of you is fired for his participation in this meeting, all the rest walk off the job and we close the mine down."

"Lucas is right," Jim declared. "If we're not willing to stand shoulder to shoulder on this, then there's no point even discussing it. You all know that the only way we've gotten improvements in the mines in the past is to speak with one voice and back up our words with actions. It's time to do that again."

"Look at how many of you showed up this evening," Lucas pointed out quietly, "despite the short notice and Wilcox's threats. What did you come here for if you're not willing to act?"

That was a challenge they could not ignore. The men shifted restlessly, glancing at each other. Slowly a consensus began to form. Carly could feel the surge of energy reaching to every corner of the room, banishing the fatigue and hopelessness, bringing in their place the determination at least to try to make their situation better.

"Just one question," a short, stocky man in the front called out, "what's in this for you, Murdock?"

In the silence that followed that demand, Carly held her breath. How Lucas answered would be crucial to the success of the effort. If the men got the idea he was offering them his help as charity, they would walk out and not look back.

He faced them steadily, his manner relaxed and confident. "Nothing, except the satisfaction of paying back something to the community where I grew up." A slight grin curved his mouth. "Some of you may remember I was a bit of a hell-raiser."

As the men laughed, he added, "Heck, some of you were right in there with me. We had good times and we didn't much think about tomorrow. Now a lot of you have families of your own. You have to think of the future. I'm here to stay and I don't aim to let my hometown be taken over by a no-good like Wilcox. So I'll fight him, and those of you who want to join me are welcome."

He had struck exactly the right note of calm determination. As a wave of approval swept through the room, Carly beamed. Deep inside, she knew he was taking on a battle many another man had tried and failed to win. But she believed he could do it. She believed he could do anything.

CHAPTER TEN

"What's this I hear about some of the men meeting with Lucas Murdock yesterday?" Pa asked over breakfast the next morning.

Carly glanced up wearily from the oatmeal she was trying to eat. It had been a long, tiring night and now she felt the effects of it. After the meeting wound down, she had parted from Lucas reluctantly, wishing they could spend the night together but knowing such a luxury was still impossible.

Heading home, her mind full of what had just happened and what it might mean for the future, she had hoped to get to bed early. Instead her sleep had been interrupted shortly after midnight by a frantic call from a young man whose wife had gone into premature labor with their first baby. There had been no time to get Sue Hendricks to a hospital. Carly had delivered her little boy shortly after dawn, as relieved by the swift birth as the mother herself.

The memory of that tiny bundle of new life she had held in her hands such a short time before still warmed her. She caught herself imagining Lucas holding a child of their own making and missed her father's question.

Pa cleared his throat, glancing at Tim and Will, who raised their eyebrows meaningfully. "Maybe you should take off today and get some rest, honey," Seth Hanlon said gently. "You look about done in."

His quiet concern reached through the haze of Carly's preoccupation. She blushed slightly, glad no one could see into her thoughts. "I'm fine, Pa, really. Besides, I have patients to see."

He frowned, not missing the look that flitted across his daughter's face but not quite able to place it. Seth sighed inwardly. She was no longer his little girl, hadn't been in a long time. But he was damned if he wanted her involved in anything that might one day hurt her.

"Seems like you're using that infirmary for more than just seeing patients," he said a bit gruffly. "How did that meeting with Murdock happen to be held there?"

Carly stifled a sigh. She was aware of her mother standing at the stove frying eggs, yet not missing a word. At the other end of the table Gram seemed occupied with her church circular. But she, too, was fully tuned in to their conversation. Will and Tim were making no secret of their interest. "It was the logical place," she said at last. "Since the men were concerned about being seen going into Lucas's office, I volunteered the use of my place."

As they continued to watch her in silent disapproval, her back stiffened. Glancing at her brothers, she asked, "Why didn't you two show up? You've worked in the mine long enough to be worried about what Wilcox is doing."

Tim looked away, unwilling to meet her eyes, but Will went on the defensive. "I'm surprised you'd even bring that up," he growled. "You know we don't deal with Murdocks."

Carly couldn't restrain a snort of impatience. She put her coffee mug down with a thud. "That's exactly the attitude the mine owners have counted on for decades. Divide and conquer. Keep the locals involved in petty feuds so they can't get organized against anything that's really important." Ignoring the startled looks from her mother and grandmother, she stood up impatiently. "If that's the way you want it, fine. But don't expect me to go along. The safety of the men in the mine is too important to let anything get in the way of improving it."

"And you really think Murdock can do that?" Will demanded. "He doesn't know beans about the mine, or the men in it. And he cares less!"

"That's not true," Carly insisted, her hand on the doorknob. "He worked in the mine every summer he was in high school. In case you don't remember, he got hurt down there. Lucas knows the dangers as well as anyone. The difference is he's not afraid to try to do something about them."

Will flushed angrily. "Afraid?"

"You heard me. You're looking for excuses to avoid getting involved. The fact that Lucas is a Murdock is mighty convenient for you. I just hope you smarten up soon, big brother. Times are changing and attitudes like yours are more than obsolete."

Not waiting for his answer, she stormed out, her face flushed and her body trembling. She hated arguing with her family, but their position was intolerable. She couldn't believe they would sit by and take no part in the struggle to improve working conditions in the mine simply because Lucas was leading the struggle. Surely they were better men than that.

The morning passed in a blur. She saw a dozen patients, paid a visit to the bank to make a deposit, coped with endless paperwork, and ordered additional supplies. By afternoon her head hurt and she was regretting not having eaten more than a few spoonfuls of oatmeal for breakfast.

Maybe a sandwich would help. Locking up the infirmary, she headed down the street toward the Modern Luncheonette. A pair of worn-out truck drivers occupied a booth toward the back and a couple of regulars were perched on their usual stools at the counter. Otherwise the place was empty.

A plump, good-natured waitress greeted her. "Hi there, Carly. How you keeping?"

"Fine, Fanny. Your arches any better?"

The older woman winced, then grinned resignedly. "A bit. You were right about soaking them every night, and the new shoes help too. But let's face it, you do this kind of work, your feet hurt. That's the breaks."

Carly nodded, accepting the plastic-covered menu she knew by heart. "How long have you been at it now?"

"Let's see . . . I started right after Ma came down with the pleurisy so that would be . . . fifteen years next month. Doesn't seem possible they've gone by so fast."

There was a hint of melancholy in her voice at the thought of lost years and all that might have been, but Fanny was no more given to pitying herself than anyone else in the Hollow.

"What the heck, it's not a bad life. I see plenty of friendly faces and just between you and me"—she leaned forward slightly, drawing Carly into a friendly ring of feminine conspiracy—"Jeb's cooking has gotten a mite better over the years. Take today for instance, the meat loaf is actually tasty."

Carly laughed but shook her head. "That's what you said about last week's chicken stew. I'll stick to tuna on whole wheat, thanks all the same."

"No sense of adventure," Fanny grumbled good-naturedly as she scribbled down the order.

The luncheonette had filled up a bit before Carly finished her belated meal. By the time she resisted Fanny's offer of a slice of lemon meringue pie, several more truckers had arrived and a couple of locals were sipping Cokes while playing the ancient juke box.

A glance outside showed the clouds were rolling in from the northwest, bringing the promise of snow that night. She was reluctant to leave the warm, friendly enclave to trudge back to the infirmary, but duty called. Sliding from her stool, she was about to take her check over to the cash register when the door was pushed open and two men strode into the luncheonette.

Both were tall and powerfully built; one was in his fifties with the weathered features of a man accustomed to decades of hard work, the other was young, about mid-twenties, but with the same confidence and strength as his sire. Both had raven-black hair. The elder's was shot through with silver. Twin pairs of crystal blue eyes stared at her, pinning her where she stood.

Lucas's father and brother—with the possible exception of herself, they were the two people closest to him in the world. The family she had to win over if she was to have any chance of a future with him.

Carly took a quick breath, forcing herself to show no hesitation before them. She handed Jeb her check as she nodded pleasantly. "Good afternoon, Mr. Murdock . . . Jared. Nice to see you."

"I'll just bet it is," the older man growled. "I've been

meaning to have a word with you, girl. Now's as good a time as any."

A barely perceptible stir rippled through the luncheonette. Even those who had no idea of the identity of those they were watching could sense the strain between them and wondered what was about to happen.

Jeb handed Carly her change nervously. He was a short, rotund man who intensely disliked trouble, especially when it happened on his property. His voice rose an octave as he called, "Fanny, bring Mr. Murdock and Jared here a couple of menus." Glancing nervously at the new arrivals, he suggested, "Why don't you two gentlemen sit down and have a bite to eat. We've got some real good pie today."

The men ignored him. As Jared continued to watch her quietly with those eyes that were so uncannily like Lucas's, his father took a step forward. "I've got a bone to pick with you, girl. What's this about you getting my boy involved in that trouble at the mine?"

The question was so unexpected that it left Carly groping for an answer. She stared up at the older man in surprise. "You aren't seriously suggesting anyone could get Lucas to do something he didn't want to do, are you?"

Eben Murdock frowned at that. He hadn't expected her to show such spirit, nor had he remembered her being quite so beautiful. His frown deepened. The little Hanlon girl had grown into a woman able to turn any man's head, even that of his eldest son.

"Sounds like you know him a bit better than you ought to," he challenged.

Despite herself, Carly couldn't help but blush. She looked away nervously. Her eyes met Jared's even as he fought a losing battle against a grin that would not be suppressed.

Choking back what sounded suspiciously like a laugh, he laid a hand on his father's shoulder. "Pa, I think maybe we better take Jeb up on that offer of pie. Maybe you'll find it just what the doctor ordered to sweeten your disposition."

Carly told herself she must be imagining the note of understanding in his words, but she couldn't be sure. Eben Murdock grumbled, but he didn't disagree. He was looking at her curiously, as though confronting a possibility he had not yet considered.

Jared smiled at her rakishly. Carly tried hard to look stern, but couldn't manage it. He was so much a younger version of Lucas, with the same male strength overlying inner tenderness. "I'm beginning to understand where my good brother's been keeping himself lately," he murmured, so quietly that only she could hear him.

"He's very busy," she insisted, a bit reluctantly. She didn't like misleading Jared. Not that she had to worry about that, since she had no chance of succeeding.

"Now how would you know that," the younger man asked ingenuously, "unless you've been keeping him company?"

The deepening flush that spread over her high-boned cheeks brought a rumbling laugh from him. It lingered behind her as Carly cast a last harried look at Lucas's kin and prudently withdrew.

Back outside on the street, she took a deep breath. The encounter had shaken her, forcefully bringing home her complete inability to think of any Murdock as a foe. The need for their approval and acceptance gnawed at her. She wanted them to see her in the best possible light, as a suitable partner for Lucas.

It was just as well that she had little time to dwell on personal problems throughout the rest of the day. A visit to check on Sue Hendricks and her new-born son was followed by house calls on several patients too ill to come into the office. The battered jeep got a workout on the twisting roads of the Hollow as she made her way to homes nestled in deep ravines and perched high on hillsides.

At each stop she was met with unfailing courtesy and gratitude. Whatever undercurrents of suspicion about her might still have existed in people's minds could not overcome their desperate need for the help she offered. There was deep satisfaction in the knowledge that she could make a difference to these people.

But there was also sorrow. She had to tell a man the X rays she had taken a few days before confirmed he had the dreaded "Black Lung," the scourge of miners and almost invariably fatal. He took the news stoically, but she drove away knowing there would be little she could do to ease either his suffering or that of his family.

Back in the office, she forced herself to go through the familiar routine of filing reports and updating patient charts. The task soothed her a little, easing some of the tension that had accumulated throughout the day.

Her thoughts were returning to the encounter with Eben and Jared Murdock when the brief rap of knuckles against the back door alerted her to Lucas's arrival. He strode in, looking devastating as usual but tired. The gray pinstripe suit he wore told Carly where he had been.

They shared a quick, sweet kiss before he flopped down in the chair near her desk and ran a hand through his hair. "That Wilcox is every bit as much a bastard as the men said."

Pouring him a cup of coffee, Carly asked, "He refused to reinstitute safety measures?"

Lucas nodded glumly. "Not only that, he made it clear he meant what he said when he warned the men not to consult me. I pointed out to him that he has no legal grounds to fire someone just because they sought legal counsel."

"What did he say to that?"

"He laughed in my face." Lucas shook his head ruefully. "I've run up against guys like him before. They think if they threaten loudly enough, everyone will do what they want."

As he sipped the coffee, Carly studied him. There were shadows under his eyes, and the lines around his mouth and on his brow were deeper than usual. But not for a moment did she believe Wilcox's attempts at intimidation would have any effect on him.

Quietly, she asked, "Will the men stand behind you?"

"If I didn't think so, I wouldn't have agreed to help them."

"Then there'll be a strike?"

He sighed deeply. "It looks that way. Wilcox will have to be convinced he's not going to get away with this. The only way to achieve that is to make him look bad in front of his bosses."

Carly didn't like the sound of that. She had seen the mine manager around town a few times and thought he looked like a hard, uncaring man with a deep fount of anger in him. He reminded her for all the world of a schoolyard bully who would never fight fair.

"Lucas . . . are you sure you want to get involved in this?"

He looked at her quizzically. "That's an odd question for you to ask."

"It's just that . . . I ran into your father and brother today, and it's clear they're concerned about you."

She hadn't meant to tell him of her encounter with his family, but it just slipped out. Lucas stood up, crossing the short distance between them, and holding out his hands to her.

Carly went to him unhesitatingly. Drawn against the solid warmth of his chest, she felt exquisitely safe and cherished. The thought that she might somehow lose that sent a tremor of fear through her.

"Sweetheart, there's nothing to be worried about," he murmured tenderly. "So long as we're together, I can cope with anything." His tone hardened slightly as he asked, "What did Eben and Jared say to you?"

"Nothing, really," she assured him hastily. The last thing she wanted to do was to cause trouble among the Murdock men. "Your father was a little upset because he thought I'd gotten you involved in the problems at the mine. I guess he's right, in a way."

"That's nonsense. I was looking for a way to get involved. You just provided it."

"I suggested that to him," she admitted. "He . . . he said I seemed to know you pretty well."

At that, Lucas was silent for a moment before laughing softly. "He's right, but I'm surprised he admitted how close we've become."

"I don't imagine he likes it," Carly said ruefully. "Fortunately, Jared drew him away before we could say anything more."

"Did my kid brother behave himself?"

The idea of that tall, commanding man as anyone's kid brother provoked a smile. "Oh, yes . . . I get the feeling he might not think too badly of me."

Lucas snorted disparagingly. "Jared has never thought

badly of a beautiful woman in his life." Gruffly, he added, "He'd do well to remember who you belong to."

Carly looked up at him in surprise. "Ignoring for a moment that rather chauvinistic phrase, you can't really believe Jared would try anything with me. It's obvious he loves you."

"I suppose so . . ." Lucas admitted, relenting slightly. "But I don't plan on taking any chances." His arms tightened around her as he grinned provokingly. "I'm going to keep you far too satisfied even to notice another man."

Her hazel eyes darkened slightly as warm ripples of anticipation washed through her. "Oh, really? And just how do you intend to do that?"

"Simple," he replied, his seeking mouth pulling gently at the delicate lobe of her ear. "By reminding you, frequently, that you belong to me."

"There's that phrase again . . ."

"You know what they say: Possession is nine tenths of the law."

"Possession," she informed him pertly, if a bit breathlessly, "is a two-way proposition."

He raised his head for a moment, crystal blue eyes meeting hers with a look that turned the ripples of warmth to liquid fire. "I possess you, you possess me?"

"Exactly." She gasped softly as his lips found the sensitive hollow at the base of her neck, his tongue making little forays into it. "As a matter of fact, from a strictly physiological point of view, I'm the one who does the possessing."

"Sounds good to me," Lucas rasped. His hand reached out unerringly to find the coat she had slung over the back of her chair. Draping it over her shoulders, he steered her toward the door. "I can recommend a very nice couch next door."

"All the comforts of home."

"Not quite, but we're getting there."

Perhaps they were, Carly thought dreamily, but she didn't mind the stops along the way to paradise.

CHAPTER ELEVEN

Paradise was both more than and less than the world. The hours in Lucas's arms made the times apart all the colder and more barren. Carly got through them moment by moment, yearning to return to the sweetness of their private joy.

Their office tryst the evening before had been gloriously passionate but too brief to satisfy either of them. They needed the golden seclusion of the cabin to give full rein to their passions.

Yet Carly had to wrest with her conscience when he asked her to join him there again. Her conflicting loyalties—to Lucas and to her family—were becoming increasingly difficult to cope with.

For a few days a spate of flu saved her from having to make a choice. She remained on night call and was summoned out several times to aid the young and the elderly, who were most susceptible to the illness.

By the time the brief bout of high fevers and stomach disorders was over, she could no longer deny her need.

Slipping out as she had before, she met Lucas at the cabin.

He was already there, waiting for her. As she stepped through the door, he rose, standing tall and dark against the fire. To her he looked almost otherworldly, a being of incomparable strength yet also capable of the greatest gentleness.

He proved that now as he embraced her tenderly, holding her so close that she felt certain some of his enormous vitality must be flowing into her.

She needed it badly; the last few days had drained her energy. Lucas seemed to sense that, for he sat her down before the fireplace and insisted that she rest and eat.

Though she claimed to have no appetite for food, Carly found herself enjoying the impromptu picnic. They dined on hearty mushroom soup poured from a Thermos and thick roast beef sandwiches on fresh-baked bread.

For dessert, Lucas produced a chocolate cake and offered her a mouthful from his fingers, not unlike a groom. "Try this. It's great, if I do say so myself."

Carly was too comfortable to argue. Somewhere in the course of the meal most of their clothes had been removed, and they were snuggled together under a blanket. The feel of his hard, warm body so close to her own encouraged an uncharacteristic sense of submissiveness.

She swallowed obediently and closed her eyes to savor the flavor better. "Hmmm . . . that's delicious. Where did you get it?"

"I made it. Out of a box. Simple."

"You're a man of many talents."

He dropped a light kiss on the tip of her nose. "That's what I've been trying to tell you."

"Oh, I get the message all right. I'd have to be crazy not to."

A gentle finger traced the curve of her cheek. "I like it when you're crazy." He laughed softly at her blush.

Several times now she had made love to him with all the consummate skill and ardor any man could ever ask for. Yet she could still be embarrassed by a teasing reminder of her own sensuality.

Carly stirred restlessly in his arms. He made her feel so discombobulated. With him the world turned upside down and inside out. Emotions she had never expected to experience held sway over reason and logic.

She was prey to sudden shifts of mood; elation at the mere sight of him, despondency when she thought of all the difficulties they faced.

Was that what love meant—living on the knife edge of sensation, never sure what the next moment would bring? She might be able to cope with that, if only temporarily, but there were other even more unsettling effects. Beneath all the fluttery hopes and ill-formed dreads there was a rock-bottom determination that what was happening between them would somehow have to work out right. If only because she couldn't live with the alternative.

She loved Lucas with all the previously untapped passion of her ardent nature. The joining of their bodies was only the most outward sign of their spirits' communion. She needed to share everything with him, including her worries.

"Did your father or Jared say anything about seeing me the other day?"

His hand tightened slightly on her shoulder in an unconscious response to her question. "Yes," he admitted reluctantly. "Eben mentioned it." He hesitated a moment before adding, "He wanted to know just how involved I was getting with you."

"What did you tell him?"

"The truth."

Carly sat up abruptly, heedless of the blanket falling away from her or of the sudden rush of cool air touching her bare skin. "Just like that, without discussing it with me first?"

"What was there to discuss? I've never lied to my father and I wasn't about to begin now."

She shook her head dazedly, not understanding how he could have been so open about their relationship. "You should have been a little more discreet."

Lucas snorted disparagingly. "You mean I should have tried to evade the issue? No thanks. This nonsense about the feud has gone on far too long. Our families are just going to have to accept the way we feel about each other."

Though he spoke with unyielding firmness, his gaze was gentle. Her distress did not escape him. He regretted having taken her by surprise, but not for a moment would he have changed what he had told Eben. His father's response had only confirmed what he already believed.

"You might be interested to know," he said quietly, "that Pa took it very well. He certainly wasn't surprised, and while he didn't fall all over himself with delight, he did allow as to how you were a good-looking woman with spirit."

"How nice of him," Carly drawled, ignoring the pleasure she felt at the older Murdock's approval. Dismay at what he had done abruptly took the lid off the fears she had pushed aside over the last several weeks, bringing them to the forefront with devastating intensity.

Coldly, she demanded, "But then why shouldn't he have said that? He probably figures you're just getting me out of your system."

The sudden flare of anger deep in Lucas's eyes and the harsh grip of his hands on her arms warned her she had gone too far. His mouth tightened ominously. "What the hell is that supposed to mean?"

Pride refused to let her back down. Defiantly, she said, "Just what it sounds like. For all your father knows, you're just sowing a few wild oats. Of course he approves."

Some hitherto unsuspected urge to provoke him prompted her to go even farther. "In fact, I'll bet he thinks it's great that you're doing it with a Hanlon."

The dark, unsettled side of their relationship, which she had managed to ignore, would no longer be denied. It loomed before her starkly, taunting her with her vulnerability to him.

Her response was completely instinctive. Resenting the hold he had on her, both physically and emotionally, she struggled to get free of him.

Lucas's hard hands tightened further. He loomed over her, big and angry and unrestrainedly masculine. "So you think I'm just using you, is that it?" he asked. "Let me tell you something, lady, I sowed all the wild oats I needed to a long time ago. You should be damn grateful I didn't do it with you."

As she opened her mouth to protest, he went on ruthlessly. "That summer before you left I came close to taking you a dozen times. You were ready, Carly, whether you want to admit it or not. I wouldn't have had any problem convincing you. But I didn't try, because you were so damn young and innocent, with your head full of dreams. I couldn't bear to do anything that might hurt you. So I lay awake night after night, aching for you, and learning to live with the fact that you were going away, that I might never see you again."

Coming down on top of her, holding her helpless underneath him, he demanded, "Do you have any idea what that felt like? I imagined you with other men, marrying someone, having his kids. I kept hoping some other woman would free me of you, but none ever did. After all that, you have the nerve to tell me I'm using you?"

Stunned by the pent-up emotions she had so carelessly unleashed, and by the revelation of how long he had truly wanted her, Carly couldn't respond. She lay beneath him wide-eyed and apprehensive, struggling to come to terms with what she had just learned.

"Lucas . . ."

"Shut up," he growled harshly. "Don't talk any more. I've got a better use for your mouth."

His proud head swooped, capturing her lips with wild demand. One hand captured both her wrists, pulling her arms taut above her head. The other moved inexorably to take her breast, closing over it with a possessiveness that stunned her.

Her soft gasp gave him the opportunity he wanted. His tongue plunged into her mouth, seizing the territory he already knew so well. Swept away by waves of sensation, Carly struggled desperately for self-control.

She held her legs tightly together, resisting the probing demand of the hard male thigh that sought to make a place for him in the warm intimacy of her softness.

Lucas raised his head, laughing at her defiance. "You can't win, you know," he muttered thickly. "You like this too much."

"Damn you! You've no right—"

"Yes, I do! We belong to each other. I won't let anything come between us, including your screwy fears and insecurities." Again his thigh probed, even more insistently. "Let me in, sweetheart," he crooned. "You know how good it will be for both of us."

"No! I won't! You think you can get round me so easily . . . make me do anything . . ."

"Why not? You have the same power over me. We're equals, Carly. There's no using going on here, only loving."

All the fight went out of her abruptly. His voice throbbed with warm sincerity, his eyes glittered with ardent need. It was impossible to doubt the truth of what he said.

A low sigh escaped Carly as the tension eased from her, leaving her soft and pliant in his hands. She shifted slightly, moving her legs apart.

He groaned huskily even as he moved to take what she offered. His entry was swift and fierce, stripped of his usual care. "I'm sorry," he muttered when they were one. "I don't want to hurt you."

"You didn't," she assured him breathlessly, her hips arching to meet him. Gentleness was not what she needed right now. Her body cried out for the full power of his maleness.

He made a valiant effort to go slowly, but Carly would have none of it. She was more than ready for him. Their earlier lovemaking and their brief struggle had brought her emotions to the flash point. Deliberately, she tightened around him, shattering his self-control.

Lucas moaned as he began to move within her, driving them both higher and higher with relentless power until at last the world shattered around them.

Long, sweet moments later when they had reluctantly

drifted back down to earth, Carly stirred in his arms. Her voice little more than a husky purr, she murmured, "Remind me to get mad at you again sometime. The results are fantastic!"

Leaving Lucas that night was harder than at any time before. They parted by the lake, sharing a last, lingering kiss before heading off in opposite directions. "I hate this," he muttered. "It has to stop soon."

"I know. You're right. When the problems are settled at the mine, then we'll tell my folks. Okay?"

"I suppose," he assented reluctantly. "But no longer than that."

She nodded and forced herself to leave his arms. The cold struck her instantly, making her shiver as she turned away and started up the path toward Hanlon land.

She turned once, to find him watching her as she knew he would be. He looked so alone standing there in the predawn light, yet also so strong and decisive—a man she could truly share her life with in perfect confidence that he would never disappoint her.

Yet she felt she had let him down somehow by insisting that they wait a while longer before springing their news on her family. It wasn't that she thought them any less resilient than Eben Murdock, only that she knew the parents of daughters were more protective than those of sons.

They would be worried about her. She needed to come to terms with that and to think of a way to soothe their fears before telling them her news.

Slipping into the house, she was relieved to find it wrapped in the hush of a new day that had not yet begun. Her parents were still asleep in their room at the head of the stairs.

Timmy and Katie would be snuggled together at the opposite end of the house. Will might be up already since he was an early riser, but at least he hadn't yet stirred from his room in the separate wing of the house. That left Gramma, who tended to sleep lightly.

On tiptoe Carly headed toward the stairs. A floorboard creaked under her, making her wince. She shook her head wryly, struck by the absurdity of a grown woman sneaking in. Lucas was right; it had to end soon.

The thought of what it would be like to spend an entire night with him, to wake in his arms and to know the joy of greeting a new day at his side, brought a smile to her lips.

She sighed softly, only to smother the sound quickly with her hand as she glanced toward the room behind the stairs where Gramma slept.

The door was open, revealing the bed already neatly made. Carly stopped where she was, aware suddenly that she was not alone.

"Seems to me you're working too hard, young'un," her grandmother informed her from her perch near the fireplace. "Coming in at this hour with your clothes all rumpled and bits of straw in your hair gives a body leave to wonder what lengths you have to go to for a bit of doctoring."

Resignedly, Carly turned toward the tart, but unexpectedly amused voice. "Good morning, Gramma. How are you feeling today?"

"Fit as a fiddle. Don't try to change the subject. What you doing coming in at this hour, girl? Your ma and pa think you've been abed for hours." Wise old eyes studied her knowingly. "Maybe they aren't too far wrong about that."

"Gramma, I—" She broke off, not knowing what to

say. The thought of losing her grandmother's respect was unbearable. Caught in so compromising a position, she seemed in danger of exactly that.

"Don't work yourself into a lather, child." Rising with the difficulty of age, she leaned on her cane as she studied her granddaughter. Eyes as green and gold as Carly's own sparkled mischievously. "Whoever he is, I'd say he's taking good care of you."

"Gramma!"

"Don't be so shocked, girl. You think you young folks invented anything?" She chuckled reminiscently. "Not likely. Now come on into the kitchen with me. We're overdue for a talk."

Carly followed reluctantly. She felt singularly unprepared to face her grandmother, whose keen intelligence and perception were in no way dulled by age.

Confronted by one who knew her so well, she understood why Lucas had told his father the truth. Attempts at evasion were as futile with Gramma as they were with the elder Murdock.

Poking sticks of kindling into the cast-iron stove, the elderly lady said, "Child, you remember when you were a real little girl and something would happen to confuse or trouble you? You'd come to me and I'd try to make sense of it for you. Maybe I didn't always succeed, but you knew you could always tell me the truth, didn't you?"

Carly's throat tightened as she nodded. "Yes . . . you never judged me. Not that Ma and Pa did really, but they can't be blamed for having expectations of their children. You always took me just the way I was."

"That's right, and I plan to go on doing that. So suppose you tell me what's going on in your young life?"

"I'm not sure where to begin . . ."

Sitting down at the wide trestle table, Gramma smiled gently. "You could start with his name."

Hesitantly, Carly took a chair opposite her. "Actually, that's the last place I'd start. First let me tell you that he's a wonderful man and I love him with all my heart."

"That's good," her grandmother murmured dryly. "Do you like him as well?"

"Of course. I just said that I—"

"Love him. That's fine, best thing in the world. But for pure day-to-day living, it helps to like each other too. Do you?"

"Yes . . . he's been my friend for years. I didn't realize how much I'd missed him until I saw him again."

"Hmmm . . . sounds like you've been carrying a torch, girl."

Carly laughed softly. "I guess I have been." Her eyes shone as she said, "Gramma, I really do love him. We belong together. It's just that . . ."

"Just what, honey? Lucas is a fine man. Any woman would be proud to call him her own."

Her granddaughter's open-mouthed astonishment prompted a warm chuckle. "You may be able to pull the wool over your ma and pa's eyes, but not mine. All those years you and Lucas snuck off to meet each other, I prayed something good would come of it." She nodded in satisfaction. "Now it finally seems my prayers were heard."

"I had no idea. I thought that if anyone found out about Lucas and me, it would cause trouble."

Gramma sighed, getting up again to pour the coffee. She waved Carly back into her seat. "I'll get it, child. While there's still life in these old bones, I like to keep moving. Now, where were we . . . Oh, yes, trouble. Well, I'm not denying if your folks had found out what was going on back when you were a young'un they would have raised hell. But it's different now. You're a full-grown woman who's proved she can make her own decisions."

"Do you really think they'll see it that way? Ma and Pa are bound to be surprised, but Timmy and Will . . ." She shuddered slightly, thinking of what her brothers would make of the situation.

"Pay them no mind. Sure they'll get their dander up, but that's to be expected. You're their sister and they love you. Lucas will just have to win them over." The wise old eyes twinkled again. "Think he can do that?"

"Yes," Carly said softly. "I'm sure he can. If he'd had his way, we would already have told my family. But at least his father knows."

"Eben? I always thought he was a right fine man. Tough but fair. Seems to me he'd welcome a chance to stop this foolishness about the feud."

Carly took a sip of her coffee, looking at her grandmother over the rim of the cup. "Is that how you really feel about it? All those generations of Hanlons and Murdocks hating each other and it was nothing more than foolishness?"

"Maybe in the beginning there was reason for bad feelings," Gramma admitted. "After all, Duncan Murdock got Judith Hanlon with child and refused to marry her. Instead he went off and got himself killed at Gettysburg, with Judith following him only a few months later when she died giving birth. A sorry tale all around, yet not something to shape our lives today."

"That's what I've always thought, but you have to admit the trouble with Duncan led to all sorts of other problems with the Murdocks. It was a cumulative effect, one incident building on top of the others to keep us at each other's throats."

"And now it's time for that to end," Gramma declared. She was quiet for a moment, turning inward to her memories as she did more and more often before rousing herself back to the present.

"I've always wondered about Duncan," she said softly. "He and Judith were both hot-tempered, passionate people. They seem to have been very much in love. It doesn't make sense that he'd leave her to fend for herself."

"Maybe he just didn't want the responsibility of a wife and child," Carly suggested.

"If that were the case, he could have said the baby wasn't his. But he never did that." Gramma set her mug down thoughtfully. "The Murdocks insist to this day that he wanted to marry Judith the moment he found out about the baby, but she held off."

"Why would she do that?"

Gramma shrugged. "It seems that there was already trouble between the families over a stretch of land near the lake that both families claimed. Judith hoped the problems could be settled before she and Duncan wed."

"Then why did he join the army of the North, knowing he might be away for years."

"Oh, he didn't do that. He just went to fight in the one battle. I suspect he hoped his absence would make Judith reconsider and agree to wed him as soon as he returned. Only he never did."

"So she was left with the babe and an outraged family," Carly said softly.

Gramma's wise old eyes were full of sadness. "Perhaps she would have died in childbirth anyway, but I can't help believing she was pining for Duncan and wanted to be with him. I hope the Lord let them be together with their child in a better place."

"I hope so too," Carly murmured thoughtfully. This was the first time she had heard the full story of Judith and Duncan, and it gave her pause to think.

Judith's insistence on waiting to tell their families in the hope that circumstances would improve had been a tragic mistake. Was she herself making the same error?

Looking up, she found Gramma watching her. "You told me this for a reason, didn't you?" Carly asked softly.

The elderly woman nodded. "There's trouble coming to the Hollow, child. I can feel it. This man Wilcox who runs the mines now cares for nothing but himself. He knows only one law—force."

Carly's throat tightened. "Lucas and the other men are determined to stand against him."

"Then the Lord be with them, child. They have a battle ahead of them." Gramma reached across the table to pat her hand gently. Looking down at the gnarled, blue-veined fingers lying on top of hers, Carly thought of all the years her grandmother had seen, all the upsets and sorrows.

Only a strong woman with a resilient spirit could have surmounted them all. Gramma looked at the world honestly, accepting it on its own terms. If she said there was trouble coming, chances were she was right.

Carly's hand tightened around her grandmother's. They sat in silence at the kitchen table as the sun rose above the eastern hills and a new day began in the Hollow.

A glance out the window showed that it was crisp and clear, the sky a pure cobalt blue dotted by only a scattering of cotton-puff clouds. Hard to believe that somewhere out of sight a storm was brewing. Yet such upheavals had swept the Hollow before, invariably bringing bloodshed and tears.

Not this time, Carly prayed, even as a cold sense of dread began to seep through her and the memory of Judith's mistake loomed before her mockingly.

CHAPTER TWELVE

For all its uneasy beginnings the day unfolded normally enough. Carly worked at the infirmary, visited patients, did all the usual things that by their very familiarity soothed her somewhat.

Yet apprehension remained strong within her. Try though she might, she could not shake it off. As she moved around town, she saw she was not alone in her worry.

At Pearson's General Store and the Modern Luncheonette, people were speaking gingerly of what was happening. Opinion was divided. Some felt the men who had met with Lucas were right. Others believed they were going too far. But both sides were clearly girding themselves for the worst.

Business was off at Maybelle Lane's Beauty Salon and at the Luxor Theater. Hairdos and movies were luxuries people could do without when there was a good chance a work stoppage might occur.

Women were still out shopping, but they were buying less. They had started checking their pantries, figuring how far the food they had put up at summer's end would stretch.

Perhaps the most telling evidence came from the children. Displays of dolls and other toys were no longer attracting much of their attention. They walked by solemn-faced. That disturbed Carly the most. It wasn't fair that the children should be affected, but it was inevitable.

Though she hadn't seen Lucas all day, she knew he had gone to see Wilcox again in a last-ditch attempt to talk sense into him. Word had spread around town that the mine manager was still intransigent, and the possibility of a work stoppage loomed larger.

Too keyed up to concentrate, she got in the jeep and drove out toward the mine. The first shift was just ending. Men emerged from below ground tired and dirty, their faces grim. They spoke quietly among themselves and with the men on the second shift waiting to replace them.

She could make out those who had been most outspoken at the meeting moving from group to group. Some received them quietly, nodding their agreement. Others argued, often vehemently. It was clear there was no consensus.

Where was Lucas? Straining her neck, Carly tried to find him. When she failed to do so, she wondered if he had gone back inside for a final attempt to make Wilcox see reason. Surely nothing else could explain his absence.

The four-o'clock whistle blew as the gates to the mine swung open. A few men moved forward. But many others stayed where they were, held back by the force of their own convictions or the persuasion of those standing with them.

Several foremen came to the fence and talked with the men. A few more passed through the barrier. The rest remained in place. There was no sign of Wilcox, though Carly thought she saw a shadow behind the venetian blind of his office.

The gates slammed shut. The men who had chosen to work walked stiffly toward the mine entrance. Those on the other side of the fence made no attempt to leave.

They milled around, talking among themselves and watching the door of the main office building. There were no shouts or catcalls, only silent condemnation and regret tinged by the understanding of what causes men to make harsh choices.

Timmy and Will were two of those who had come out of the mine at the end of the first shift. They saw her waiting in the jeep and came over to join her.

"Been here long, Sis?" Will asked quietly.

She shook her head. "No, I just came to see . . . what would happen."

"It hasn't yet," Timmy reminded her. "This is only the beginning."

There wasn't much to say to that. He was right, of course, but she didn't want to think about it. Instead, she asked, "Are you going to work tomorrow, if this isn't settled?"

Will shrugged. He glanced at his brother as he said, "This isn't an authorized strike."

Carly's mouth tightened. "So what? The union representatives were at the meeting with Lucas."

"Only unofficially," Timmy pointed out. "The union itself isn't involved."

"Which brings up an interesting point," she said. "Why isn't it?"

Will raised the collar of his sheepskin jacket, his shoulders hunched against the wind. "This is a small mine without a whole lot of employees. The union prefers to concentrate on the big guys. They figure they can do the most good that way."

"But they're still supposed to represent you, aren't they?"

"Yes, and maybe if they see this is more than just talk, they'll get involved."

"If you wait for that . . ."

"We'll have to think about what we're going to do," Timmy said firmly. "One thing's for sure; we're not anxious to follow any Murdock. I don't trust them any more than I do Wilcox."

Carly bit her lip as she listened to him. His stubborn refusal to think of the Murdocks as anything but enemies strained her patience to the limit. Forcing herself to stay calm, she asked, "Do you think Lucas was wrong to encourage this?"

Will hesitated barely an instant before he shook his head. "No, much as I hate to say a good word about a Murdock, he did the right thing. Conditions down there are so bad that even a delay of a day or two could mean injury or death." Grimly, he added, "I just hope that he can carry through and get some good out of it."

They left her a few minutes later, heading back to their car for the trip home. Carly waited a while longer, hoping for a glimpse of Lucas, before she reluctantly started back to town. She had a few more stops to make before calling it a day.

Sue Hendricks was last on her list of house calls. The new mother and her child were doing so well that the visit wasn't absolutely necessary. Carly made it for her own sake as much as theirs.

Sitting in the small but well-appointed house with the baby on her lap, she let herself forget for a moment what was going on at the mine and concentrate instead on the new life she had helped bring into the world.

"We're so grateful to you," the young woman said as she gazed up at her husband. He sat on the edge of the bed, his arm around his wife, looking considerably better than the last time Carly had seen him.

Gently, she teased the nineteen-year-old boy who seemed to have changed overnight into a man. "You've settled down a mite, Hank. For a while there I thought I was going to have three patients instead of two."

He blushed, but took it good-naturedly. "I'll tell you the truth, Doc, I was scared out of my wits. When the baby started coming, all I could think of was that I'd have to get old Ma Fester or one of the other women who midwife. But I didn't want that for Sue. Then I recollected you'd come back."

He shook his head at the memory. "You can bet my hand was shaking the whole time I was dialing your number. Why I had to do it twice before I got it right!"

Carly joined in the laughter following this abashed recollection, but her expression was serious as she said, "There's nothing wrong with midwives, Hank, if they're properly trained and have access to good medical facilities. Ma Fester doesn't qualify on either count."

"There used to be no alternative," Sue pointed out gently. "Women were glad of any help they could get." Her face clouded as she added, "And so many of them died trying to birth their babies. Thank God those days are finally over!"

Carly was still thinking about that as she started the drive home. It was rather telling that Hank had never considered calling the emergency medical facilities at the mine. But then they weren't much good to start with and had never been used for anything other than accidents occurring right on mine property.

Wilcox's appointment as manager had only emphasized what had always been mine policy; the workers should fend for themselves and be grateful for whatever scraps were thrown their way.

Times were changing, at long last. People were no longer content with marginal lives. They were standing up for themselves and demanding improvements. Such resolution was admirable, but didn't change the fact that the struggle was by no means over.

Deep in thought, Carly almost missed the turnoff to the lake road. She took it carefully, mindful that after dark the going was rough. A full moon sailed over the lake, illuminating the roof of the cabin and reminding her of how she and Lucas had made love the night before.

A blush stained her cheeks as she shifted restlessly behind the wheel. The need to see and touch him had become an ache inside her. The day now finally passing seemed to have gone on forever.

Even if he was too busy to spend any time with her, she had to find some way to talk with him. Otherwise, sleep would be impossible.

Lights were on at the Murdock house. She could see them clearly. Pulling over to the side of the road, she hesitated a moment. Why shouldn't she go see Lucas? Eben and Jared knew about her; they could hardly be surprised by her arrival.

Granted, she might not be welcome, but she doubted they would be so foolish as to try to throw her out, at least not if Lucas was there. And if he wasn't, they would most likely know where she could find him.

Turning the jeep around, she headed back down the road toward the other side of the lake. Barely a mile lay between her home and Lucas's, but the distance might have been far greater. She had never before been this far onto Murdock land.

The house she finally pulled up in front of stood at the end of a long gravel drive framed by big old oak trees. In the moonlight she could make out the shape of a building similar in style to her own home, but larger and more luxurious. The ramshackle quality of a house that had been added on to over the generations was replaced by elegant graciousness.

Vaguely she remembered that when careful management of their land had made the Murdocks rich, Eben had torn down the haphazard additions and replaced them with a structure true to the family's heritage but in keeping with its new-found wealth.

The core of the original homestead still stood, bracketed by large wings set aside for the families he hoped his sons would one day sire. So far neither Lucas nor Jared had obliged him.

The lights she had seen from across the lake all shone in the main part of the house. As she drove up, the door was flung open. A figure loomed there, large and masculine. As she got out of the jeep gingerly, it moved toward her.

"How did you get here so fast?" Jared demanded. His face was tight and strained, and the good humor she had noticed about him earlier was gone. In its place was a grim urgency she could not understand. Before she could answer, he went on hurriedly, "Never mind. There's no time to waste. Where's your bag?"

"Bag?"

Seeming not to have heard her, Jared stepped toward the jeep. The medical bag in the backseat caught his eye. He snatched it up and turned toward the house.

Instinctively, Carly followed him. "We've managed to stop most of the bleeding," he said grimly. "But he's hurt bad and being out in the cold for who knows how many hours sure hasn't done him any good."

A dizzying sense of dread washed over Carly. She shouldn't have known what he was talking about, but somehow she did. Dazedly, she murmured, "Lucas . . ."

"When Pa called your place and they said you were out, we thought we were really in for it," Jared said as he hurried her up the stairs. He paused for a moment before a closed door. Looking down at her, his eyes were bleak. "They told the truth, didn't they, Carly? You weren't there? I'd hate to think even Hanlons would want to deny us help in these circumstances."

Tight-lipped, she reminded him, "I'm a Hanlon, Jared."

He shook his head. "You're different."

"No, I'm not. That's the whole point. But this isn't the time or place to discuss it." Taking a deep breath, she steeled herself for what lay ahead. "Let's go inside."

Something flashed behind his eyes—sympathy, perhaps—then it was gone as the door swung open.

Eben glanced up from his vigil beside the bed. He looked old and tired, as if he were struggling to cope with a mortal blow. Carly had only an instant to perceive the harsh evidence of his fight in his weathered features and the taut set of his still-powerful body before her gaze shifted to the man on the bed.

For a moment she didn't recognize Lucas. Both of his eyes were swollen closed, and blood caked his nose and mouth. Bruises and abrasions covered his bare shoulders and chest as far as she could see above the blanket spread over him. One arm was outflung; the hand lay palm upward with the vulnerability of a sleeping child. But Lucas was not asleep; he was unconscious.

Carly bit back a cry of horror. To see him like that ripped away the fragile fabric of her self-control and threatened to turn her into an anguished creature of mindless outrage.

But before that could happen, her professional training clamped down on her. She moved toward the bed numbly, automatically seeking out the telltale signs of injury and trauma. Setting her bag on the table, she began to take out what she would need.

"When did you find him?"

If Eben found her expressionless tone surprising, he did not show it. Instead, he took a ragged breath before saying, "Some men outside the mine got worried when they couldn't find any trace of him. They called me, then started looking. His jeep was found over by the main road and we tracked him into the woods. Looks as though he was waylaid while heading for the mine. There were a bunch of them—five, maybe six. They got him out of sight and . . . did this . . ."

Carly's hands shook slightly as she lifted the blanket away, but otherwise she gave no sign of what she was feeling. What little color was left in her face vanished as she took in the evidence of his suffering.

Livid bruises covered his chest and abdomen. Without touching him, she guessed that several ribs were likely to be broken and there might well be other internal injuries. Ignoring the cold rage washing over her, she asked, "Has he been conscious at all?"

Eben shook his head. "We kept hoping he'd come to so he could tell us who was responsible. But so far there hasn't been a flicker out of him."

Under the circumstances that might be best. If Lucas

were conscious, he would be in acute pain. Lacking information about a possible head injury, she couldn't sedate him. For the moment she had to hope that his condition did not indicate anything more serious than a simple concussion.

With gentle hands, she examined him carefully. The beating had been thorough. Hardly an inch of him remained unbruised.

"Have you called the police?"

Jared took a step closer to the bed, his hands clenched at his sides. "Yes, but it won't do much good. I don't think they're any too anxious to get involved in this."

"They're not going to have any choice," Carly said quietly. "As a doctor, it's my responsibility to file a report of criminal assault." She stared down at the man lying so still in the bed. "Two ribs are broken, so is his left wrist. There may be other fractures, but without X rays I can't be sure. He should be at a hospital."

Jared and Eben glanced at each other worriedly. "It's twenty miles to Branchville over rough roads."

Carly stifled a sigh. "I know, and he can't be moved safely until his condition has stabilized. We'll have to wait. In the meantime I'd like one of you to go to the infirmary and get some supplies for me."

Sitting down in a chair beside the bed, she made a quick list. "The IVs and oxygen are in the closet of the examining room. You'll also find a locked cabinet there for drugs. Here's the key. I'll need antibiotics and a few other things."

She didn't add that one of the drugs on the list was Adrenalin. If Lucas's internal injuries were as bad as they might be, a heart seizure was not out of the question. In that event, she would need every tool in her small arsenal to keep him alive.

Jared hurried off and moments later she heard the roar of a car engine. The sound faded away down the road as she put her fingers over Lucas's pulse, constantly monitoring it as together she and Eben kept a silent vigil.

Within half an hour Jared was back with everything she had requested. The supplies came none too soon. Lucas's breathing had become labored as she slid the oxygen mask over his nose and mouth and inserted the IV. His color was gray tinged with blue.

He was suffering as much from the effects of exposure as from the beating itself. The only cause for optimism lay in the slow but steady beat of life beneath her fingers.

"How . . . is he?" Eben asked hesitantly.

Carly respected the older man too much to lie to him. "Not good, but he's holding his own. All things considered, he's lucky to be alive."

"No thanks to those bastards who jumped him," Jared hissed angrily. He stared down at his brother intently, as though seeking to impart his own strength to him.

"Do you have any idea who they were?" Carly asked.

A pulse leaped in Eben's throat. "Goons Wilcox hired, I suppose. There's never been any shortage of muscle for hire around here."

"It might not even have come to that," Jared pointed out. "Maybe some of the men who didn't support the strike decided to do something to stop him."

"I can't believe that," Carly interjected quickly. "Sure there are men who weren't happy about the confrontation and wanted to end it. But that's a far cry from almost killing someone."

"It's not so unlikely," Jared insisted. "We've done too well for ourselves as a family not to make enemies. Jealousy and spitefulness are powerful motivations."

The room fell silent. Unspoken among the three people

grouped around the bed was the acknowledgment that if anyone disliked the Murdocks enough to attack one of them, it was the Hanlons. Timmy and Will had even been reluctant to support the work stoppage because Lucas was involved.

Not for a moment did Carly believe they could have taken part in the attack against Lucas, but she feared his father and brother might believe that was at least a possibility.

In an effort to derail what might be the train of their thoughts, she asked, "Jared said something about you calling my place?"

"Your pa wasn't any too happy to hear from me," Eben said shortly. "Near snapped my head off saying you weren't there, then slammed the phone down in my ear."

"I imagine he was surprised to hear from you," Carly murmured. She had no difficulty picturing the scene after that phone call: her father baffled and worried, Will and Timmy adding their own concerns, her mother fretting over where she might be, and Gramma . . . ? Gramma would have kept her own council, revealing no confidences but steering them all in the direction she thought they should go.

And just where would that be? Would her grandmother insist that Carly was fine, and they should all calm down and wait for her to come home? Or would she see an opportunity to bring about the face-to-face meeting that she had long believed essential to settling the feud?

That possibility sent a flare of near panic surging through Carly. It was all too easy to imagine Gramma quietly suggesting they'd best find out what business Eben Murdock had with a Hanlon girl. The best way to do that—indeed, the only way pride would allow—was to beard the lion in his own den.

Even as she told herself she was letting her imagination run away with her, Carly knew with icy certainty that she had anticipated events by no more than scant minutes.

Through the window of Lucas's room she could see the lake road along which she had traveled a short time before. Once again headlights were moving down it from the direction of Hanlon land. They were coming fast, and straight toward them.

The confrontation she had dreaded for so long was at last about to occur.

CHAPTER THIRTEEN

"What are you doing here, Carly?" Seth Hanlon demanded. He stood on the porch of the Murdock house, his arms folded across his chest and his face tight. Behind him Will and Timmy were similarly disposed.

Her brothers' anger did not surprise her, for they were young and given to extreme emotions. But the sight of her gentle father in such a state took her aback.

For a moment she considered reminding him that she was a doctor and went where she was needed. But that would be dishonest. At any rate she had no opportunity to answer. Eben did it for her.

"She's here caring for my son, Lucas." He pulled the door open farther and gestured for them to come inside. "You've come this far, you might as well go the rest of the way." A humorless grin curved his mouth. "Unless you're scared, that is."

Will took a quick step forward, confronting him. "We're not afraid of you, Murdock. Find somebody else to look after whatever ails Lucas. Come on, Carly, we're leaving."

Standing at the foot of the stairs, the farthest she was willing to go from the man lying so still in the bed upstairs, she stared at her brother in mingled disbelief and outrage. "I'm not some child you can order around, Will Hanlon, and I'll thank you not to try to run my life. Now if you've come to help, fine, otherwise you'd best take yourself off right now."

Meeting the startled looks of her father and Timmy, she added, "That goes for all of you. There's trouble in this house. We don't need any more."

"Trouble?" Seth Hanlon repeated slowly. He wasn't sure what had come over his daughter, or how to cope with it. But he saw more than she knew. Her eyes were bright with unshed tears and her slender shoulders trembled slightly.

He could read the fear lying like a cold stone within her, and for a moment thought that Eben and Jared were responsible. His natural reaction was even greater anger, but not so great, however, as to block out his common sense. The two Murdock men looked no better than Carly. Something was truly wrong.

Taking a step toward her, he asked quietly, "What's happened, child? Tell me."

Armored against his anger, she could not resist his gentleness. Barely aware of what she was doing, Carly went into his arms, her head against his chest as a sob was wrenched from her. "Oh, Pa, it's Lucas. He's so badly hurt. I'm afraid he'll . . ."

Over her head Seth met Eben's anguished eyes, surprised when he could find no grain of comfort in his old enemy's suffering. Instead there was only the common bond of fathers made helpless by the vulnerability of their children.

A low sigh escaped Seth Hanlon. It was a soft sound,

hardly earthshaking, but evidence nonetheless of the final dissolution of a dark chain that had bound him and Eben and too many other Hanlons and Murdocks in a generations-old feud.

The film of grief clouding Eben's eyes cleared slightly. In the way of men of similar age and experience, he recognized what was happening to Seth.

There was no mistaking it, since the same process was going on within himself. Swallowing hard, he murmured, "Let's go on upstairs. Lucas shouldn't be left alone."

"There's no reason for them to be up there," Jared protested, gesturing to the Hanlon men. He was protective of his brother and didn't like the idea of anyone who did not love him seeing him as he was now.

Yet even as he spoke, his objection gave way before the certain knowledge that love was present. What his brother had found with Carly seemed strong enough to bind up many wounds.

Seth and his sons followed Carly and Eben up the stairs, with Jared coming last. The door to Lucas's bedroom was open, as she had left it. A muttered exclamation escaped Seth as he saw the mute evidence of savagery.

Will flinched slightly, but did not draw back. Only Timmy remained by the door. What barroom brawls he had witnessed in his young life had not prepared him for the effects of so concerted an effort at destruction.

It took a moment for Seth to recover sufficiently to speak. Hoarsely, he asked, "Who did this?"

"We don't know for sure yet," Eben said. "Probably goons hired by the mine manager. We'll find out."

No one had to ask what would happen once the identity of Lucas's assailants became known. The police would have a chance to intervene, but if they did not act speedily, justice would still be done.

Seth stood a while longer beside the bed, his weathered features tight with compassion and regret. Any such attack would have prompted his outrage, no matter who the victim was. But being a father of sons himself, he needed no leap of imagination to know what it would feel like if one of his boys were lying there.

When he turned back to Eben, his eyes were hard with determination. "You'll need help." Without giving the other man a chance to object even perfunctorily, he went on, "Will and Timmy, you'll notify every man on the first shift of what's happened. When that mine opens this morning, the picket line should be ten deep with absolutely no one crossing it. Got it?"

His sons nodded and were about to leave when Jared called them back. "Wait, you'll make better time if you take two cars." Pulling the keys to his out of a pocket, he handed them to Will. The two looked at each other for a moment, before Will abruptly nodded. Gesturing to Timmy, he said, "Let's get going."

When they were gone, Seth addressed himself to Eben. With scrupulous courtesy, he asked, "If I may use your phone, I'll call my wife."

Surprised, Carly broke off her scrutiny of Lucas momentarily. "Are you sure you want to involve Ma?"

Her father nodded firmly. "She'd never forgive me if I didn't. Besides, she's needed here."

Within a matter of hours Carly understood what he had meant. Rachel's arrival brought a quiet sense of hope and purposefulness to the besieged household. She wasted no time establishing herself in the kitchen, from which quickly began to waft wholesome aromas of soup and fresh-baked bread.

When Carly at last fell into an exhausted sleep on the bed beside Lucas, it was her mother who covered her with a warm quilt and stood looking down at the pair for long moments, her soft face suffused with tenderness. It was Rachel who ignored Eben's and Jared's protests that they weren't hungry and insisted that they eat.

She held sway with gentle strength that left the Murdock men, who were unused to a woman's care, slightly dazed, but appreciative.

Carly woke toward midday, sitting up quickly to check Lucas. Some of the tension ebbed from her as she realized he was breathing more easily and his color was returning.

Automatically she renewed the IV and gave him another injection of antibiotics. She thought he stirred slightly under her touch, but wasn't absolutely sure.

Men came and went from the house all afternoon. The police, an older man and his young deputy, finally arrived, abashed at having brushed off Eben's earlier concern and now determined to do their duty, if only because they knew the alternative would be a return to frontier justice. They left after talking with Carly and learning what she could tell them of the type of weapon used.

The union representative at the mine was next. He was a quiet man more given to resignation than action. But the events of the last few days had made him think there might be hope after all for a solution to the problems plaguing the men who looked to him for leadership.

Having come to that conclusion, he was not about to give it up. The attack on Lucas stiffened his backbone to an unprecedented degree. He went off thinking how it might have been him lying there, and vowed that those responsible would pay.

Throughout the day one of those rare convergences of local events and larger objectives began to unfold. The powers that be at the union, who until then had been content to have no involvement beyond their single representative, decided it was time to put their own stamp on what was occurring in the Hollow.

Always hungry for something to fill air time, the networks were quick to pick up on what was happening, especially since the union men pointed out that many strikes had occurred in the Hollow, but years had passed since a spontaneous shutdown shook the hills.

A vivid tableau was being played out before the chain-link fence guarding the mine: men outraged at the contempt authority had for their lives, and determined in the name of decency and honor to right the wrong done to them and theirs.

The bait was irresistible. It was theater and it was reality—the perfect combination to attract the omnipresent eye of the people, national television.

On the third night, just as attention might have begun to slack off a bit, a newsman for one of the major networks finally got through to Eben and convinced him to grant an interview.

The elder Murdock did so reluctantly. He didn't like the idea of exposing his grief and rage before the public, yet he was too realistic not to know that such publicity could be the best possible guarantee of Lucas's safety.

Slowly his son was beginning to rally. As Carly hovered over him, never leaving his side, the shadow of death began to recede. Eben rejoiced at that, but did not try to deny what it meant.

Once Lucas regained consciousness, he would waste little time returning to the fray and placing himself once again in danger. His father was determined to assure that when he did so, he would be protected.

Eben went on television and told the nation about the

attack against his son. He spoke quietly, without histrionics. He needed none.

People saw him, heard him, and believed him. The growing public dismay at what was happening in the Hollow abruptly coalesced around a single man.

Lucas continued to sleep through it all. Carly was able to remove the IV and oxygen. She consulted with several other doctors, who flew in to volunteer their services, and agreed that hospitalization was no longer necessary. A portable X ray machine had revealed that his injuries did not extend beyond the fractures she had already identified.

His condition was headline news far beyond West Virginia. He had quite inadvertently become the symbol of a struggle that in that particular time and place had seized the public's imagination. Men and women who had never met him spoke of his courage and selflessness. There was talk of running him for office.

Carly was aware of all that, but only from a distance. Her concentration was focused strictly on the man she loved and on each small step he made toward recovery.

Exhausted by the long days and nights at his side, she prudently stopped herself from thinking too much about the future for, like Eben, she could see what lay ahead.

Part of her cried out in protest against the possibility of Lucas being further endangered. He had done enough. No one should be asked to do more. Yet she knew as surely as she loved him that he could not walk away from what he had begun.

A battle raged within Carly. The woman in her saw some good in his continued weakness, for it provided a measure of safety. But the doctor was determined to restore him to full health no matter what the consequences.

In the last few weeks she had learned that there were

times when the woman had to be given full sway. But not now. The struggle was hard but brief: the doctor won.

Early on the fourth day Lucas woke up.

Carly was seated in her usual chair beside his bed. She was very tired, yet unable to sleep. Hovering on the edge of sleep, she was instantly alert to the slightest change in him.

A subtle alteration in the rhythm of his breathing made her lift her head. She was reaching for him when his eyes suddenly flickered open and he met her gaze.

"C-Carly . . ."

"Yes, I'm here," she said, feeling happier and more relieved than she'd ever felt before. "Don't try to move around too much. You've been hurt." Her hand shook as she smoothed an unruly lock of hair away from his forehead. The professional in her automatically noticed his improved skin color and how quickly his bewilderment at returning to consciousness gave way to comprehension, but the woman saw only the return of strength and vitality.

"Those men . . ." he rasped. "They must have done a hell of a number on me." A hollow laugh broke from him as he grimaced. "I hurt in places I didn't know I had."

Carly blinked hard against the tears that threatened to blur him in her sight. With the growing certainty of his survival, a torrent of pent-up emotions threatened to burst from her. She knew she was in dire danger of drowning him in her tears, and rather than do that, she took refuge in humor.

Shakily, she told him, "You do have a rare collection of bruises."

He reached up to catch her hand in his and bring it to his lips. "I'll bet, but you're not looking any too chipper yourself. How long have I been here?"

"Three days," she admitted reluctantly, knowing what was coming.

"God! I had no idea! I've got to get up." Even as he spoke, he was trying to rise from the bed, only to find to his immense frustration that his body would not obey him.

"I think not," Carly said firmly. "You're going to stay right here until I say otherwise." As he opened his mouth to argue, she added, "You'll follow your doctor's orders or I'll give you something that will leave you no choice."

"That's not ethical," he protested, but only half-heartedly.

"No, but it sure is practical. I had a feeling that once you woke up you'd be a terrible patient, and you're already proving it." For all the sharpness of her words, they did not sting. She was incapable of being angry at him.

Lucas saw that and smiled ruefully. Taking her hand again, he drew her down on the bed beside him. "I'll make you a deal," he offered.

Carly raised an eyebrow warily. "What kind?"

His gaze ran over her, taking in the lavender shadows beneath her eyes, the paleness of her skin, and the leaden sense of weariness pressing against her slender shoulders. His mouth was tight as he said, "You've worn yourself out, no doubt taking care of me. So if I have to stay here, you do too."

Nothing sounded more inviting to her than to stretch out next to him in the big bed and feel again the security of his nearness, but Carly still hesitated. He had been gravely injured and was still in a lot of pain. The last thing he should have to do was comfort her.

"Whatever you're worrying about," he said, "forget it. Now come here."

Reluctance left her as she yielded to his compelling gentleness. Removing her shoes, she slid under the covers.

As she settled next to him, he lay back and closed his eyes, the tension easing from him. Having her in his bed in a sense renewed his possession of her. Not, by any means, to his complete satisfaction, but that, he wryly acknowledged, would have to wait.

"Go to sleep," he murmured gruffly. "Before I forget I'm an injured man."

Carly laughed softly. She could not help but comply. Already the last vestiges of the fear that had kept her going through the long days were leaving her. In their place was exhaustion deeper than any she had ever known. But there was also contentment, and above all an abiding gratitude that Lucas's life had been preserved.

Within moments they were both asleep, their heads lying together on a single pillow and their hands entwined above the covers.

Rachel found them like that when she stuck her head in an hour later to find out if everything was all right. She stood for a moment gazing at her daughter lying so naturally beside the man she had been raised to think of as an inevitable enemy.

For a moment she felt a fierce sense of protectiveness. If he hurt Carly . . . Then that thought fled and another, far greater one came to her.

Perhaps because the life she had led was close to the rhythms of nature, Rachel had a deeply imbued sense of what was fitting and what was not. Looking at the pair on the bed, she knew beyond doubt that what she was seeing—the coming together of Carly and Lucas—was part of the natural order of things. It was as inevitable as the rising of the sun and the endless cycle of nature.

Her fears for her daughter, and for her future, vanished and were replaced by a deep sense of pleasure in the eternal rightness of love. Smiling, she quietly closed the door and went back downstairs.

CHAPTER FOURTEEN

"I don't have any choice, Carly," Lucas said firmly. "I have to go down there." He was sitting on the living room couch, fully dressed and doing his best to look completely recovered.

It was barely a week since he had regained consciousness, but he was adamant that he take part in an inspection of the mine arranged by the owners. They hoped to quell the public outcry by spotlighting those few safety measures that still happened to be in effect.

"If I don't go," Lucas said quietly, "I'll be yielding the upper hand to the mine owners, and you can be sure they'll make the most of it. We're at a very delicate point in our dealings with them. We have to keep the public pressure working for us."

"You're crazy," she snapped, well aware that that was hardly a reasonable response. But reason was slipping away from her. She had been arguing with him to no avail for almost an hour. All of her most logical objections were being waved aside.

When she insisted that he was still weak and in pain

from his injuries, he denied it. When she reminded him that only a short time before he almost had died, he commended her on the splendid job she had done as his doctor. When she tried to convince him that he already had done his part for the miners, he quietly but firmly corrected her.

Whether he wished it or not, he had become the focal point of the struggle against Wilcox and the mine owners. So long as management remained intransigent, he owed it to the men on the picket line to do all he possibly could to bring them around. Otherwise, it would look as though they were all backing down.

Confronted with the inevitability of what he intended to do, Carly struggled to keep her composure. She turned away from him, hoping he wouldn't see the sheen of tears on her hazel eyes.

He wasn't fooled. Standing up, with some difficulty, he went over to her and put his arms around her. She tried to remain stiff within his embrace, but couldn't manage that any more than she could manage to stay angry at him.

"Sweetheart, it will be all right," he murmured gently. "I promise. I'll go down there with Wilcox and the TV reporters; he'll give his spiel and I'll point out all his lies and evasions. We'll give the media some great film and in the process get some hard evidence to prove our complaints. Now what's the harm in that?"

"You know perfectly well," Carly muttered, trying not to think about how hard and good he felt against her. After so many days at his bedside, mustering all her stubbornness and skill to heal him, the knowledge that his strength was returning only emphasized her own weariness and vulnerability. "It really is dangerous down there. You could get hurt . . . again."

His arms tightened around her. She felt the gentle press of his lips against her forehead before he said teasingly, "That would be like lightning striking twice in the same place. The odds must be a thousand to one, easily."

Carly was in no mood for humor. She was tired, worried, and strung out. There was absolutely no way she was going to let him make a joke of this. Drawing back, she glared at him. "Oh, that's great! Setting odds on your life! Where do I put down a bet?"

"Honey . . . you're getting upset over nothing . . ."

"Nothing? I sweated blood over you these last few days and now you want to go risk everything just to get on television!"

Lucas let her go abruptly. Beneath his burnished tan, his skin was ashen. He sat down again, carefully, on the couch. Drawing a deep breath, he said, "Carly, I could try all day to reason with you, but I doubt I'd get anywhere. I wish I could make you feel good about this, but I can't."

Looking up at her, he added softly, "What it comes down to is that I've made up my mind about what I have to do and now I'm asking for your understanding. If you can't approve, will you at least give me your support?"

Carly opened her mouth automatically, only to shut it abruptly. There were no easy answers to what he was asking. He wanted an act of faith from her, an acknowledgment that in this case at least she would put aside her own feelings for his sake.

For barely an instant she wondered if she could actually do that. She was a strong, independent woman. How could she be expected to push aside her convictions and meekly accept his?

Yet how could she not? It was really very simple: She loved him, therefore she had to be whatever he needed.

She didn't doubt that in the vast majority of disagreements that might crop up between them, they'd settle on a satisfactory compromise. But this time, with so many other people depending on him, it had to be all or nothing.

Carly's anger fled. Why was she mad at him anyway? Because he was decent and honorable, qualities that made her love him?

In the face of that love all other considerations became unimportant. Slipping to her knees before him, she embraced him. Tremulously, she whispered, "I'm sorry for acting like a shrew. It's just that . . . this business of caring for someone so much is new to me." She laughed shakily. "I'll get better at it, I promise."

Lucas groaned huskily. His arms clasped her to him. "You don't need to get better at anything. You're perfect just the way you are." With tender gruffness, he added, "I can't stand the idea of us being at quits with each other."

"We never will be," Carly vowed, pressing her lips to the pulse beating in his throat. They remained nestled against each other through long, sweet moments, until a sound from the door yanked them back into the world.

Timmy was standing there, watching them. Like the other Hanlon men, he'd been in the Murdock house often over the last few days. He'd helped to care for Lucas and rejoiced in his recovery. But that was a far cry from being pleased to find him embracing his sister.

His young face showed how he was torn with contradictory emotions: anger, bewilderment, and beneath it all the growing maturity signaled by tolerance. Carly tried to stand up, to go to him and say something reassuring, but Lucas held her in place. He refused to let her go, instead forcing Timmy to confront the truth between them.

"Something we can do for you?" he asked the younger man quietly.

"Katie asked me to drop by . . . she made a casserole for dinner." Beneath his unwavering scrutiny, Carly flushed. Her position between Lucas's thighs could hardly have been more intimate. Timmy might be her little brother, but he was man enough to recognize what that said about how well they knew each other.

"That was very nice of her," Lucas said, still unshaken. He released Carly at last and stood up. "I'll put it in the refrigerator. Can you stay for coffee?"

"Uh . . . no thanks . . . I'm due on the picket line in a few minutes." His gaze shifted to his sister. "Carly . . ."

She met his eyes bravely, determined there would be no equivocation between them. Flustered though she was to be discovered in this way, she could not deny her relief that her relationship with Lucas was finally out in the open.

Gramma, of course, had known for a while now, and Carly suspected her mother was well aware of the truth. She could hardly fail to be since she had seen for herself how Carly had suffered during the days she cared for Lucas. Though Rachel Hanlon had so far restrained herself and said nothing about the situation, her daughter was certain she wouldn't be surprised by what Timmy had witnessed.

Soon they would all have to talk about it, but not while she was still trying to come to terms with the fact that Lucas meant to go down into the mine.

"Let it go for a bit, Timmy," she said gently. "Too much is happening right now."

For a moment she thought he meant to argue with her, but instead he reluctantly assented. "You know where I'll be," he said huskily as he turned to leave.

When he was gone, Carly faced Lucas resolutely. Before he could speak, she quietly announced, "I'm going with you."

Under other circumstances, the look on his face would have been humorous. His mouth dropped open and his eyes widened. Surprise swiftly gave way to determination. "No, you are not. That's out of the question."

She raised an eyebrow eloquently. "Really, who says so?"

"I do. I absolutely forbid you to go on that inspection."

"Forbid? Where on earth did you get the idea that I need your permission to do anything? I happen to be a doctor, and if anyone has a right to go where there's danger, it's me. If trouble occurs down there, I can do a damn sight more good than you can!"

"That doesn't matter," Lucas insisted. "You're not going. It isn't safe for a—" He broke off, abruptly aware that he was stepping on very thin ice.

"A woman?" Carly finished scathingly. "I hate to be the one to break this to you, but we happen to live in the last quarter of the twentieth century. That kind of attitude has gone the way of buggy whips and hoop skirts."

"Has it?" Lucas challenged heatedly. He crossed the room in rapid strides to stand before her. His broad chest rose and fell distractedly as he demanded, "What's so wrong about a man wanting to protect his woman?"

"Is that how you think of me?" she shot back, trying to ignore the surge of pleasure those words gave her. "As just another possession? I've got news for you—"

"Don't be ridiculous!" Lucas snapped. His hands

seized her shoulders, not painfully but with firmness that told her she would be wise not to resist. "You're a part of me, as I'm a part of you. If something happened to you, I'd . . ." His eyes darkened, becoming almost bleak. "Let's just say I wouldn't be able to handle it real well. I can't stand by and let you put yourself at risk. Don't you understand that?"

"Yes," Carly said softly, looking up at him. She made no effort to get free, but instead leaned closer to him. They fit together so perfectly; she could stay like that quite contentedly all her life. "I understand. That's exactly how I feel about you. But as you pointed out, you still have to go into the mine. So do I."

Gently she pressed her fingers to his mouth to keep him from speaking. "I'm a doctor, Lucas. I took an oath to heal, and I have every bit as much responsibility to the people in this town as you do. There are dangers in the mine that I can identify and explain better than any lay person."

He gazed down at her, the struggle he was waging clearly stamped on his proud features. Very softly, she said, "You asked for my understanding and support. Won't you give me the same?"

The corners of his mouth turned up wryly. "That's not fair. How am I supposed to refuse you when you turn my own words against me?"

"You're not. That's the point."

He drew her closer, resting his chin against the warm silk of her hair. "You drive a hard bargain, woman."

The resigned acceptance in his voice made her smile. Safe within the shelter of his body, she murmured, "Then we'll both go."

Lucas nodded. "Together."

Standing at the entrance to the mine a few hours later, Carly knew the time for second thoughts was long past. A barrage of television lights illuminated the early winter gloom. One of the mine owners, a youngish and photogenic executive, was giving an interview, explaining the purpose of the inspection.

"There's been so much concern lately about mine safety that we've decided the best way to settle the issue once and for all is to open up the whole matter for public inspection. We're taking the extraordinary step of inviting a group of independent observers from the media to go into the mine with our manager, Mr. Wilcox. He'll answer your questions and give you plenty of opportunity to look around."

Gazing into the camera, he concluded, "I'm confident that by the time you come back up, you'll understand the whole issue of mine safety is a lot more complex than you've been led to believe, and you'll realize that we've been doing everything possible to insure the safety of our workers above and below ground."

"How do you feel about Mr. Murdock and Dr. Hanlon going along on this tour?" one of the reporters asked.

The executive smiled thinly. "Ordinarily, we don't encourage civilians to enter the mines. They're liable to cause damage or other problems."

"Apparently that doesn't apply to the media," Carly muttered.

"But under these unusual circumstances," the executive went on, "we've decided to bend the rules, if only to prove our sincerity."

That last blatant bit of propaganda brought a disparaging snort from Lucas. "They're sincere all right. They sincerely want to wring every possible dime out of the mine and the consequences be damned."

"What happens," the reporter was continuing, "if contrary to your expectations, this inspection turns up problems with mine safety?"

"That isn't going to happen," the executive assured the viewing audience. "This mine is safe." He gestured toward the fence on the other side of which the picket line was moving up and down in an effort to keep warm. "Those men out there have been misled. There was never any reason for them to go through all this. Whatever problems might have existed were extremely minor and have been taken care of."

"In a pig's eye!" Lucas grated. "I'm willing to bet they've made some cosmetic improvements below ground, and that's it. The real problems are as bad as ever."

"Then it's up to us to make sure the cameras see them," Carly said. She patted her hard hat and took a deep breath. The interview was winding up. The inspection was about to begin.

CHAPTER FIFTEEN

It was cold and dank in the mine. Strings of yellow lights illuminated the narrow-gauge track that led from the surface into the tunnels below. Six open carts were linked together into a rickety train that creaked and groaned down the steep grade.

"We double-checked the brakes on this thing," Wilcox called back to the reporters seated behind him. He sat confidently in the lead cart, with his hard hat pushed disdainfully back on his bullet-shaped head.

Carly had been watching him since they began the descent from the surface. A suspicion was forming in her mind, one she didn't want to believe could be true, but which refused to go away.

What exactly had Wilcox told his superiors about conditions below ground? The men who owned the mine were executives of a large conglomerate that, among other things, manufactured toothpaste and made cable TV movies. They knew next to nothing about mining coal, except what appeared at the bottom of earnings statements.

They would have had no choice but to depend on Wilcox, their chosen appointee, to give them a fair evaluation of safety conditions. Had he been so concerned about looking good in their eyes that he had glossed over the truth?

That would explain how the owners' spokesman could stand up in front of the television camera and lie so sincerely. If he had no idea he wasn't telling the truth, he'd have no reason to be bothered.

For a while there, as she had listened to him, she had come close to subscribing to the popular view that corporations cared for nothing except profits and would go to any lengths to protect them. But that was an insanely shortsighted perspective that could doom any company to ultimate collapse. No executive as coldly reasonable as the man she had seen in front of the cameras would follow such a destructive course.

As they left the carts and stood in the main staging area, dotted by tunnels vanishing away into the darkness, Carly tugged at Lucas's sleeve. As he bent close to her, she whispered, "What do we know about Wilcox?"

He frowned, unsure of the reason for her question, but said, "Not much. He's in his mid-fifties, divorced, two kids he apparently doesn't see. Used to work for one of the bigger outfits." He named a company that mined fully a quarter of all the coal in the country. "Ran into some kind of trouble there, I don't know what. He was out of work for a while before coming here."

"Anything else?"

"That's about it? Why, what's on your mind?"

"I don't know exactly," Carly admitted. "It's just that something . . . doesn't feel right."

"Of course not. There's a hell of a lot wrong down here and the company is doing its best to hide it."

"But why? Oh, I know what you said about profits and I agree that makes sense. Yet surely there has to be a point beyond which even the most rapacious mine owner won't go, at least not if he has any real hopes of staying in business."

Again Lucas looked puzzled. "So . . . ?"

"So why are they doing this? They're going to wind up very embarrassed."

"But they don't know that."

"That's my point." Drawing him a little aside from the rest of the group, Carly said urgently, "What if Wilcox lied to make himself look good? What if the owners really don't know what's going on down here?"

"That's crazy. He couldn't hope to get away with it."

"Not if he thought about it logically, but maybe he isn't capable of that. Look at him."

Reluctantly, Lucas did so. Wilcox was holding forth to the media, indulging in a bit of grandstanding in front of the cameras. He was a big man, easily six feet, but overweight and flabby. The buttons of his jacket strained across his big belly. His gray hair was thin and limp. His eyes were red-rimmed, his bulbous nose reddened by numerous broken capillaries.

"Ain't nothing wrong with this mine," he announced, chomping on a cigar left unlit in deference to safety regulations so well known even he could not ignore them. "Not one damn thing. I run a tight ship. Nothing gets past me. Why you just take a look at this alarm system here."

The camera shifted obediently as the reporters chosen from the media pool leaned forward. Briefly, Wilcox described how every part of the mine was wired for instant communication in the event of an emergency.

"Something happens, let's say over there in tunnel

number three. We can notify the men throughout the mine in seconds and, if necessary, get them started on their way to the surface."

Lucas cast Carly a quick glance. Together they stepped over toward the main circuit box that controlled the emergency-notification system. "I'd like to say a word about this," Lucas began quietly. In sharp contrast to Wilcox, his manner was cool and restrained.

"It's true this communications network is an important part of mine safety, but only when it works properly. Trouble started in the alarm system several months ago, shortly after Mr. Wilcox took over managing."

Glancing at each of the reporters, he said, "You've undoubtedly noticed it's damp down here. Wires running throughout this system have begun to rust and deteriorate. They need to be replaced. It's a simple job that costs a few dollars, nothing exorbitant. But so far Mr. Wilcox has refused to authorize it."

"Hold on there a minute, boy," the mine manager snapped. "I was asked for a complete overhaul of this system when all it needed was a few more parts. No way I was going along with that!"

"You were asked to keep the emergency system in working order for the safety of the men," Lucas said quietly. "You refused."

Wilcox looked about to argue further but apparently thought better of it. Sticking his cigar back in his mouth, he grated, "We can hassle that out later. Let's get on with it."

With minicams and reporters trailing after them, they proceeded toward a tunnel leading off toward the northeast. "Old number six here has been in constant operation for a couple of decades," Wilcox said as though he could take personal credit for that feat. "It contains one of the richest veins of coal in the whole Appalachian range. I'm proud to show it to you."

"I should think so," Lucas murmured, "since it looks as though it's gotten a real thorough going-over quite recently."

Carly could see what he meant. The tunnel was strung with brighter lights than any of those surrounding it. Signs were posted every few hundred feet reminding workers of safety regulations. Thick steel beams were braced against the walls and ceiling, giving an air of unshakable stability. The chambers where coal was currently being mined were high enough for a man to stand in comfortably, and bone dry.

"Come on this way," Wilcox called as he headed toward a bend in the tunnel. "There's something over here you've really got to see!"

A pudgy finger gestured to a length of fuse stretched over the ground and running off into the distance. "You fellows want to find out how a real mine operates, don't you? We have to blast through thousands of cubic yards of rock every day before we can get at the coal. The only way to do that is by blasting."

He grinned inanely. "Now you just ask yourselves, if this little old mine weren't safe, would I risk setting off dynamite while I was standing right here?"

Carly smothered a gasp. The fuse running away into the darkness must be connected to an explosive charge that was used to open up new veins of coal. Beneath her sheepskin jacket, she had suddenly gone icy cold. Even as she told herself he couldn't be serious, she had a sudden terrible premonition of what was about to happen.

"This has gone far enough," Lucas said flatly. He took a step toward the older man, intent on stopping him. But Wilcox's appearance was deceptive. For all his bulk, he was still capable of moving quickly. The fuse was lit before any of the reporters fully realized what was happening.

"What the hell?"

"What's going on? Is that a—"

"Hey, fun's fun, guys, but let's quit kidding around."

"This is no joke," Lucas grated as he pushed Wilcox out of the way and headed for the burning fuse. He meant to stomp it out before it could burn any farther, but the mine manager wasn't about to allow that.

"Oh, no, you don't! I said this mine was safe and now I'm going to prove it. You're not stopping me!"

Lucas ignored him; all his attention was on the fuse. So much so that he didn't hear the low, feral growl that broke from Wilcox or realize what was about to come.

Carly had no such problem. As the mine manager raised a beefy arm, she screamed and launched herself forward. In time to partially deflect the blow, but not to stop it altogether.

Lucas took a sharp blow to the kidneys as Carly was sent sprawling against the rock wall. That was enough for the reporters. Several lunged at the mine manager, while their colleagues thoughtfully kept the cameras running.

Wilcox was subdued swiftly, yet the effort was wasted. The fuse had continued burning, past the point where anyone could safely attempt to put it out. Groaning, Lucas straightened and grabbed Carly's arm.

"Come on! That thing's going to blow in a few seconds. We've got to get out of here!"

The reporters needed no greater urging. They made a rush for the tunnel exit. Lucas threw Wilcox's arm over his shoulder and began dragging him away, shouting at Carly to go on ahead. She didn't bother to respond to that. Adding her strength to his, together they pulled the mine manager along with them. The lights of the staging area could be seen, the little train waiting patiently in place, when a low rumble shook the tunnel.

The overhead lights swayed ominously and flickered. Clouds of dust and small rocks rained down from the ceiling. In a moment it was over; the ground once again was steady beneath their feet.

The reporters looked around hesitantly, hardly daring to believe their luck. One of them laughed shakily. "Maybe things aren't so bad down here, after all."

As though the mine had only been waiting for his words, a new tremor struck the tunnel. It rolled toward them from the direction of the blast, like a great wave pushing through stone. Carly watched in dazed fascination as the lights far back in the tunnel began to go out one after the other.

The knowledge of what that meant kept her glued to the spot. Her legs felt like rubber and she found she was forgetting to breathe. Shakily, she drew in air, only to choke on the heavy accumulation of dust.

"It's a cavein!" Lucas yelled. "There's no time to get out. Get down!"

Grabbing Carly around the waist, he flung her to the ground and threw himself on top of her. Her face was pressed against his chest, her arms and legs pinned beneath him.

She had a moment to meet his eyes, which were filled with anguish and indescribable yearning, before all sight and sound were obliterated in the terrible, remorseless rush of earth plummeting down to bury them in a man-made tomb.

Carly stirred gingerly beneath Lucas. The cavein seemed to be over. It was pitch black in the tunnel, and she had to pull her turtleneck sweater up to filter the air so that she could breathe. But she seemed to be alive and essentially unhurt.

Lucas? Dread spiraled through her as she struggled to gauge his condition. Only partially recovered from the beating he'd taken and still reeling from Wilcox's blow, how could he hope to come through this all right?

Desperately she twisted under him, trying to wriggle out so that she could get a look at him and determine what needed to be done. "Lucas, are you all right?"

He raised his head, shaking off the dust and grinning down at her. "Sweetheart, I keep trying to tell you I'm tougher than you think. I'm fine. How about you?"

A giddy sense of relief washed through her. For the moment all that mattered was that they were both alive and together. "I couldn't be better."

He laughed softly, well aware of what she was feeling since he shared her joy at being alive. "That's my girl. Here, let me help you up."

They rose together, dusting each other off, and glanced around. Carly pulled out a flashlight and turned it on. By its light they could make out the reporters standing up dazedly, glancing around as though they couldn't quite believe they were still alive. Some had cuts and bruises, but otherwise they seemed okay.

Wilcox was crouched in a corner. The hard hat he had disdainfully worn pushed back on his head was gone, knocked onto the ground. A bleeding gash stretched from one side of his balding pate to the other. He was moaning fitfully.

Carly went to him at once. She had no medical equipment, but she would offer what help she could. Whatever she felt for the man personally, she had a job to do.

"We've got to clear a place for him to lie down," she

said briskly. "He's suffered a concussion, possibly worse."

Lucas and the other men quickly cleared a patch of ground, then laid the burly mine manager down carefully. He was semi-conscious and blinked at them fitfully. "M-must have been a mistake . . . it was safe . . . I know . . ."

"That's enough." Lucas cut him off. He didn't like to see anyone suffer, but not for the world could he muster the slightest sympathy for the man who was responsible for their predicament.

Turning to the reporters, he pulled a flashlight from his pocket and ordered, "One of you take this and find the emergency system. See if the radio is working. The rest of you sit down. The less you move around, the less oxygen you'll use."

"Do you think we'll be down here long enough for that to be a problem?" one of the younger men asked gingerly.

"I don't know," Lucas admitted. "But if the radio isn't working, it's going to be a while before a rescue team gets through." He didn't add that there was still the possibility of further caveins that might put them beyond anyone's reach.

Carly knew that without being told. They were incredibly fortunate to have survived this long. There was no telling how long their luck might hold. Keeping a firm grip on her courage, she settled back next to Lucas and tried hard to look as calm and confident as he did.

The reporter sent to find the emergency system came back moments later. "Is the radio working?" Lucas asked him. He shook his head disgustedly. "No, it's eroded with rust just like you said. But I did find this."

Holding out his hand, he indicated a box of first-aid supplies. Carly took it eagerly, only to have her hopes dashed the moment she opened it. Only a few bandages remained. The splints, antiseptic creams, and other items that should have been in it were gone.

"There were also a couple of emergency face masks and canisters of oxygen," the reporter went on. "But the rubber around the masks is shot to hell and the pressure gauges indicate that the canisters are empty."

"Great," one of his colleagues muttered. "Now what the hell do we do?"

"Sit tight," Lucas said firmly. "That's all we can do. We'll be found. It's just a question of time."

The men glanced at each other, resisting the impulse to ask how much time he thought they had left. Abruptly, one of them laughed. As the others stared at him, he explained, "I just checked my camera. It still works. If we ever get out of here, we'll have some great film!" The others laughed uneasily.

Flashlights were turned off to conserve their batteries, and with the returning darkness silence once again descended on the chamber. Some faint light was filtering through from the staging area, but only enough to keep complete blackness at bay.

Carly leaned her head back on Lucas's shoulder, glad of his strong arm around her. She breathed slowly, concentrating on the rhythm and trying not to think. But inevitably thoughts began to stir.

Would they get out? That was a foolish question since no one could know the answer. By this time those on the surface would know a cavein had occurred and would be mustering all their resources to reach those trapped below. But there could be no guarantee that they would be in time.

How ironic that was. It did not escape her that just as all her and Lucas's problems with their families seemed on the verge of resolution, everything they hoped for might be snatched away from them.

She had been wrong to think the feud was still as powerful as it had once been. In doing so, she had underestimated both her family and Lucas's. Hanlons and Murdocks alike had grown over the years to the point where they could cherish the good the hills had to offer without being bound by the bad. They had needed only a reason to put aside the ill will between them once and for all.

Were the two families to be united not in joy but in grief? Judith and Duncan had found their place together not in the world but in the grave. Was the same to be the case for her and Lucas?

It did no good to rail against the terrible unfairness of that. If she had learned anything in her twenty-eight years, it was that life wasn't fair. At least not by any mortal measure.

As though he could read her despairing thoughts, Lucas drew her closer. So softly that only she could hear him, he whispered, "We'll get through this, sweetheart. We'll make it."

Carly wanted desperately to believe him. With all her heart she yearned to return with him to the world above, to stand again in the sun and know the joy of building a life together. She blinked hard as she thought of all the things they might yet have done: all the laughter and loving, the home they could have shared, the children she could have given him.

It might all still be real, but just then it was no more than a dream. She knew he spoke only from the desire to give her comfort, not from any true certainty. Yet in some way he was right. The tension in her body began to ease as she realized that bad as things were, they could be worse. She might have remained on the surface and been there even now, alone and terrified without Lucas.

Better to be together. No matter what the outcome.

The scraping noises began perhaps an hour later. It was hard to keep track of time in the darkness, but judging by the growing staleness of the air, they had been trapped in the chamber for upward of sixty minutes. Six pairs of lungs were quickly exhausting the oxygen supply. It was cold and so quiet every sound was amplified a dozen times over. The strike of a shovel hitting stone seemed like an explosion.

Lucas sat up, drawing Carly with him. They inched their way over to the rock fall blocking the tunnel. Pressing his ear to it, Lucas listened intently.

Hoarsely, he muttered, "There's someone there. I can hear them." Grabbing a stone, he began to bang rhythmically against the rocks. Carly did the same. Behind them the reporters began sitting up, trying to shrug off their growing lethargy and see what was going on.

The returning tap on the other side of the barrier was perhaps the sweetest sound Carly had ever heard, other than the sound of her name on Lucas's lips. He said it now, with a wide smile, as he reached out a gentle hand to brush away the tears suddenly spilling down her cheeks.

The sounds got stronger. They could hear the muffled shouts of men and the clang of picks and more shovels against the rock. Those working to free them would know time was running out. They were bringing all their strength to bear against the wall of rubble.

It got lighter in the chamber. A hole was being carved in the debris. It became wider and wider, until at last Carly could make out a face peering in at her.

"Timmy!"

He grinned at her broadly, seemingly oblivious to the fact that he, too, was crying. His young voice shook slightly as he said, "Hi, there, Sis. How's Lucas?"

From beside her Lucas answered for himself. "Fine. We're all okay, except Wilcox. He's hurt, but not too badly."

Timmy nodded, eyeing them both. As anxious hands swiftly extended the opening, he said, "You know, I've been thinking about things. Carly's always had a penchant for getting into trouble. Now it seems like you do too. Maybe you two deserve each other."

They were all still laughing when the gap in the wall became large enough for them to crawl through. Carly was first out, received in her brother's arms joyously.

She could see Will reaching in to help Lucas and Jared standing off to one side, grinning at them. But it was the two men still pulling rubble from the wall that caught her attention most forcefully. Seth and Eben were working side by side in perfect accord, as though they had done exactly that every day of their lives.

CHAPTER SIXTEEN

There was pandemonium on the surface. Television lights illuminated the mine so brightly that it might still have been day. In their glare the faces of the mine owners were pale and drained. They were men with the fight gone out of them, defeated by the simple weapon of truth so profound not even they could deny it. The gate in front of the mine was open, the picket line dissolved as everyone streamed in to help with the rescue effort. There would be no reason for it to return.

Wilcox was carried to a waiting ambulance. He looked like a broken man, destroyed by his own selfishness. Later in the hospital at Branchville he would reveal the names of the men who had beaten Lucas, and give the information needed for their arrests. But just then no one watching him being driven away really cared about that.

They all had other things on their minds. Seth Hanlon said it best when he put a friendly but very firm arm around Lucas's shoulders. He glanced at Eben humorously as he said, "I think it's time we had a talk, son.

Isn't there something you want to tell me . . . about setting a wedding date?"

Lucas smiled broadly and held out a hand to Carly. She took it willingly, gazing up at him with such unstinting love that even her father had to chuckle. "The sooner the better, son. Right?"

"Whatever you say, sir," Lucas agreed as he drew his wife-to-be closer. Smiling down at her, he added, "But you can leave your shotgun at home. Unless, of course, you think she might not want to make an honest man out of me."

Carly laughed tenderly and nestled against him. "Oh, but I do," she assured both him and their families.

A week later she said the same words in the little church where such a short time before the people of the Hollow had gone to pray for better times. They were all gathered there again, to witness the uniting of two families and the end for all time to the ancient feud.

Maybelle Lane played the organ, a bit off key but no one minded. Reverend Johnson presided and made a good job of it. Emily and Katie were the matrons of honor. Emily's baby woke up halfway through and cried a bit. Her father hushed her ably.

Carly wore her grandmother's wedding dress and her mother's veil. She carried a bouquet of late-blooming wild flowers from the hill near the lake, and she looked beautiful. No one could remember seeing a lovelier bride.

Lucas was a bit nervous. He'd been out the night before with Will, Timmy, and Jared. They'd kidded him pretty outrageously, asking if he knew what a handful he was taking on.

He did. He'd waited for her a long time, just as she had waited for him. They had come together at last against all odds, and they had found the path from darkness to the light.

When he saw her coming toward him down the aisle on her father's arm, he stopped being nervous. His voice was firm and steady as he said his vows, and so was hers.

The kiss they shared before the altar, in the sight of God and man, was long and tender. The smiles that greeted them when they turned to face the world for the first time as man and wife were filled with love. Rachel cried a little. So did Gramma. Eben and Seth managed not to.

Carly didn't mind shedding a tear as she gazed up at her husband. He was her love, the other part of herself. She faced the future at his side with complete serenity, knowing that he felt the same way about her.

But that didn't stop either of them from kicking up their heels at the wedding supper. All the women in the Hollow had contributed. Platters groaned under the weight of roasts and stews, fresh-baked bread, vegetables, and salads, and enough desserts to make the eyes of every child—and not a few adults—near burst out in anticipation.

Anticipation . . . perhaps that was the sauce that made the feast so special. All through the brightly swirling evening, as she laughed and danced and laughed some more, Carly never lost sight of Lucas. Their eyes met a hundred times in private caresses that presaged all that was to come.

When most of the groaning boards of food had been done away with it and more than a dent put in the supplies of cider, beer, and white lightnin', the fiddlers switched to a slow, dreamy tune.

Smiles fell like dewdrops on the newly wedded couple as Lucas claimed her for the dance. Nestled in his strong arms, her cheek resting against his broad chest, she drifted with him on the haunting mountain melody until the music became indistinguishable from the rhythms pulsing through their bodies.

The last strains of the fiddles had died away some moments before they realized it and came abruptly back to earth, or at least as close to it as they could manage. Both looked abashed as the wedding guests chuckled knowingly.

"Better take her off, son," Seth said. "There'll be other parties for you two to linger at."

They needed no further encouragement. To the delight of all assembled, Lucas swept her into his arms, the train of her white silk and lace gown cascading around them, and carried her with swift strides toward the door.

A shower of rice and good wishes followed them to his car. Carly had a brief moment to squeeze her father's hand and kiss her mother before Lucas slid behind the wheel. With a final wave and teary smiles, they drove off in the direction of the lake road.

The silence was broken only by the softly wafting breeze and the sound of lapping water. The excitement of the party faded swiftly, replaced by the far deeper exhilaration of being alone.

"I'm glad we decided to stay at the cabin," Carly murmured. She sat almost primly with her long gown hiding her legs and her hands folded neatly in her lap.

Lucas cast her a glance that was at once tender and predatory. "By the time Gramma and Rachel got through with it, they'd turned it into a palace."

Carly laughed in agreement. "How they managed along with the wedding preparations I'll never know. But don't forget Pa and Eben, they helped too."

"They fixed all the leaks in the roof and replastered all the walls to keep out the drafts."

"It just won't be the same place anymore," she murmured teasingly.

Her husband grinned, rather wolfishly. "Don't be so sure about that, Mrs. Murdock. I think you'll find one or two things haven't changed."

"Oh, really, what could that be?"

By way of an answer Lucas pulled in beside the cabin, strode swiftly around to her side, and lifted her from the car. As he turned toward the door, Carly protested half-heartedly. "I hope you don't plan to go on hauling me around like this."

"It might be a good idea. At least that way I'll always know where you are."

She giggled softly as he pushed open the door and carried her inside. "It would be a little hard to explain to your clients and my patients. Not to mention those men who want you to run for office."

Setting her gently on her feet in the center of a large braided rug, Lucas looked down at her somberly. "I know we've talked about this already, but are you really sure you wouldn't mind?"

Without hesitation she nodded. "I'm sure. We have so much, we can't keep it all to ourselves. Eventually I'd like to see a whole network of clinics set up wherever they're needed."

Her hands went to work on the buttons of his white silk shirt as she added, "If you get elected to the state house, maybe you could help me build that network."

"You wouldn't think of bribing me?" he asked hopefully.

"Actually, that's just what I'm planning to do." She

unfastened the last of the shirt buttons and parted the material to get access to the furry breadth of his chest.

Lucas sucked his breath in. Thickly, he said, "I warn you, it won't be easy."

"Nothing worthwhile ever is," Carly murmured, dropping feather-light kisses from his collarbone to the flat male nipples that hardened at her touch. Huskily, she added, "But I'm very determined."

"You always were stubborn . . ." His voice trailed off, ending in a husky groan. Her hands had found the button of his waistband and made short work of both it and his zipper.

Very intently, as though tackling a difficult and essential task, Carly undressed him. She slipped the jacket and shirt from his shoulders and laid them over a nearby chair. Her gentle push was enough to convince him to sit down on the edge of the bed. Kneeling so that her veil hid the curve of her cheek, she removed his shoes and socks, then with determination tugged him back onto his feet.

Lucas was smiling, rather crookedly. His eyes were smoky with desire. Glancing up, she saw an overwhelming tenderness that made her breath catch in her throat.

"You're so lovely," he murmured, cupping her chin in his hand and tilting her head back. Their lips touched in a slow, seeking kiss that only increased their hunger.

Trembling, Carly pulled back. "Don't distract me. I've got those clinics to think of."

He grinned and raised his hands in surrender. "Far be it from me to get in the way of a good bribe."

"Good, then stand still." He did as he was told, with the result that his trousers and shorts quickly landed on the floor. Stepping out of them, he kicked them away and faced her unabashedly naked and aroused.

"What a scene we must make." Carly laughed. Her hand swept down the line of her sumptuous bridal raiment. "Me like this and you . . ."

He took a step toward her, his smile lazy and sensuous. "We'll just have to remedy that."

Slowly, as though he had all the time in the world, Lucas undressed his wife. First he removed her delicate veil and placed it carefully out of harm's way. Laying his hands on her shoulders, he turned her until her back was to him. One by one he undid the tiny seed-pearl buttons, all two dozen of them, stretching from the nape of her neck to the curve of her buttocks. Before he had finished, she was visibly trembling.

"Easy," he rasped. "We have all night." Turning her again, he eased the gown from her shoulders and arms, baring the high curve of her breasts covered only by a lacy camisole.

To step out of the dress Carly had to lean against him. At the first touch of his warm rough-silk skin she gasped softly. The strength seemed to go out of her legs so that by the time her dress had also been laid carefully aside, she could barely stand.

By the firelight she watched him return to her, all taut and golden in the dancing flames. The planes and angles of his magnificent body were cast into sharp relief, reminding her of some ancient sculpture come to life.

But no mere work of marble could ever equal his power. Through him flowed the very force that sparked the universe. Deep within her, the core of her own power pulsed with need.

"Lucas . . ."

"Hmmm . . ."

"Don't you think we should . . ."

"Should what, sweetheart?" he murmured caressingly

as his fingers eased beneath the waistband of her ankle-length slip, sliding it down her legs until it lay in a pool of satin at her feet.

She watched him bemusedly, savoring the wide sweep of his shoulders and back as he knelt before her, gently removing her slippers. When she wore only her camisole and panties, he rose and studied her intently.

Beneath the hot sweep of his gaze she blushed. Her nipples grew hard and taut, and in the secret woman's place at the cleft of her thighs a honeyed moistness gathered.

Yet when she would have ended the torture by drawing off the rest of her clothing, Lucas stopped her. He lifted her onto the bed, then lay down on top of her and slowly, deliberately smoothed the silk over her breasts.

"Beautiful . . ." he muttered as he bent his head, his tongue flicking over first one swollen bud and then the other. Carly gazed down at herself bemusedly. The dampened fabric clung to her, more erotic in a way than complete nudity.

Lucas thought so too. His big hands grasped her waist, holding her still for him, as he continued his enthralling torment.

Not until she was writhing beneath him, moaning helplessly, did he at last slide the straps from her shoulders and push the delicate silk down until her full, aching breasts were bared. They throbbed for his touch, but he withheld it.

Turning on his back, he drew her to him. Her glistening chestnut hair spilled down on either side, framing the piquant loveliness of her features. As she moved against him, he gasped. "Sweet witch . . . I wanted to make this last."

Carly laughed deep in her throat. She had too, but that

hope was gone, eclipsed by the remorseless strength of their need. "Later . . . we'll have all the time in the world . . ."

He nodded, his eyes smoky with desire. Neither of them could delay any longer. The arching tumescence of his manhood pressing against her belly sent waves of yearning crashing through her. The last barriers between them fell away. With instinctive skill, she moved to bring him within her.

Lucas gasped. His big hands closed round her breasts, squeezing and kneading tenderly. Carly moaned, her head falling back. Firelight danced over her alabaster skin, turning it to molten gold. He gazed up at her, seeing her at that instant as some otherworldly being who held the very essence of him in deepest thrall.

Masculine pride made him assert himself. His hips rose; he drove himself more fully into her, then out again, repeating the rhythm countless times until Carly cried out.

"No more . . . I can't stand it . . ."

"You can," he rasped. "You will." They were both slicked with perspiration, and their breath came in pants as the forces gathering within them neared their crescendo.

Carly's hands pressed against his chest, her fingers becoming entangled in the thick mat of hair. The musky scent of love sent her senses spinning. Her body rose and fell with his, holding the pace, drawing out the ecstasy until at last the whirlwind seized them both and they were lost to anything but incandescent pleasure.

So profound was their release that they slipped from the pinnacle of ecstasy into sleep still intimately knit together. Their rest was brief. Carly returned to awareness to find herself stretched out on her side next to Lucas. He was facing her, his gaze infinitely tender, as his manhood moved within her once again.

This time they took it more slowly, altering the rhythm, brushing up against the peak only to retreat some little way. Several times Lucas stopped moving altogether, letting her powerful inner muscles drive them both higher and higher.

Carly managed a breathless laugh when he did that yet again. "Lazy . . ."

"On the contrary," he gasped, "indulgent . . . I want you to know how strong you are."

"Not just me . . . both of us . . ." The convulsive ripples were beginning again, making it impossible for her to speak. Her hands entangled in his hair, her lips met his in a kiss of infinite tenderness.

Whether it was the deep undulations of the velvet nest that sheathed him, or the aching sweetness of her mouth on his, or simply the unbridled force of his need, Lucas did not know. But he was thrillingly aware that she was driving him to a peak of rapture he had never before experienced.

For an instant he tried to hold back. Then the futility of that, and the needlessness, struck him. He watched, enthralled, as Carly yielded to her own release. Her back was arched, lifting her breasts against him. Her eyes turned to sea-green flames and the soft flower of her mouth opened to emit a cry of utter joy that was his name.

He had less than the space of a heartbeat to savor his triumph before the explosive force of his seed pulsing into her signaled that in this battle there were no losers, only victors.

A long time later, when their dazed senses at last began to clear, Lucas thought to pull the covers over them.

Carly nestled lovingly against him. Sleep claimed them both.

In the depths of night the fire fell away into embers. Outside the darkness sang with the silver sounds of rustling pine trees and fluttering wings. Moonlight peered through the shuttered windows, spilling across the bed where a man and a woman lay secure in each other's arms.

An owl called and the wind answered. As it always had from the beginning of time in the mountains. As it always would, until time itself ceased and only love remained.

LOOK FOR NEXT MONTH'S
CANDLELIGHT ECSTASY ROMANCES®:

290 BALANCE OF POWER, *Shirley Hart*
291 BEGINNER'S LUCK, *Alexis Hill Jordan*
292 LIVE TOGETHER AS STRANGERS, *Megan Lane*
293 AND ONE MAKES FIVE, *Kit Daley*
294 RAINBOW'S END, *Lori Copeland*
295 LOVE'S DAWNING, *Tate McKenna*
296 SOUTHERN COMFORT, *Carla Neggers*
297 FORGOTTEN DREAMS, *Eleanor Woods*